TELL ME TO STOP

CHARLOTTE BYRD

CHARLOTTE BYRD

dangerously addictive

Identifiers

- Tell Me to Stop (Hardcover): 978-1-63225-052-0

- Tell Me to Stop (Paperback): 978-1-63225-051-3

- Tell Me to Stop (eBook): 978-1-63225-050-6

❀ Created with Vellum

PRAISE FOR CHARLOTTE BYRD

"BEST AUTHOR YET! Charlotte has done it again! There is a reason she is an amazing author and she continues to prove it! I was definitely not disappointed in this series!!"
★★★★★

"LOVE!!! I loved this book and the whole series!!! I just wish it didn't have to end. I am definitely a fan for life!!! ★★★★★

"Extremely captivating, sexy, steamy, intriguing, and intense!" ★★★★★

"Addictive and impossible to put down."
★★★★★

"What a magnificent story from the 1st book through book 6 it never slowed down always surprising the reader in one way or the other. Nicholas and Olive's paths crossed in a most unorthodox way and that's how their story begins it's exhilarating with that nail biting suspense that keeps you riding on the edge the whole series. You'll love it!" ★★★★★

"What is Love Worth. This is a great epic ending to this series. Nicholas and Olive have a deep connection and the mystery surrounding the deaths of the people he is accused of murdering is to be read. Olive is one strong woman with deep convictions. The twists, angst, confusion is all put together to make this worthwhile read."
★★★★★

"Fast-paced romantic suspense filled with twists and turns, danger, betrayal, and so much more." ★★★★★

"Decadent, delicious, & dangerously addictive!" - Amazon Review ★★★★★

"Titillation so masterfully woven, no reader can resist its pull. A MUST-BUY!" - Bobbi Koe, Amazon Review ★★★★★

"Captivating!" - Crystal Jones, Amazon Review ★★★★★

"Sexy, secretive, pulsating chemistry..." - Mrs. K, Amazon Reviewer ★★★★★

"Charlotte Byrd is a brilliant writer. I've read loads and I've laughed and cried. She writes a balanced book with brilliant characters. Well done!" -Amazon Review ★★★★★

"Hot, steamy, and a great storyline." - Christine Reese ★★★★★

"My oh my....Charlotte has made me a fan for life." - JJ, Amazon Reviewer ★★★★★

"Wow. Just wow. Charlotte Byrd leaves me speechless and humble... It definitely kept me on the edge of my seat. Once you pick it up, you won't put it down." - Amazon Review ★★★★★

" Intrigue, lust, and great characters...what more could you ask for?!" - Dragonfly Lady

★★★★★

WANT TO BE THE FIRST TO KNOW ABOUT MY UPCOMING SALES, NEW RELEASES AND EXCLUSIVE GIVEAWAYS?

Sign up for my newsletter: https://www.subscribepage.com/byrdVIPList

Join my Facebook Group: https://www.facebook.com/groups/276340079439433/

Bonus Points: Follow me on BookBub and Goodreads!

ABOUT CHARLOTTE BYRD

Charlotte Byrd is the bestselling author of romantic suspense novels. She has sold over 1 Million books and has been translated into five languages.

She lives near Palm Springs, California with her husband, son, a toy Australian Shepherd and a Ragdoll cat. Charlotte is addicted to books and Netflix and she loves hot weather and crystal blue water.

Write her here:

charlotte@charlotte-byrd.com

Check out her books here:

www.charlotte-byrd.com

Connect with her here:

www.facebook.com/charlottebyrdbooks

www.instagram.com/charlottebyrdbooks

www.twitter.com/byrdauthor

Sign up for my newsletter: https://www.subscribepage.com/byrdVIPList

Join my Facebook Group: https://www.facebook.com/groups/276340079439433/

Bonus Points: Follow me on BookBub and Goodreads!

facebook.com/charlottebyrdbooks

twitter.com/byrdauthor

instagram.com/charlottebyrdbooks

bookbub.com/profile/charlotte-byrd

Tell me Series
Tell Me to Stop
Tell Me to Go
Tell Me to Stay
Tell Me to Run
Tell Me to Fight
Tell Me to Lie

Wedlocked Trilogy
Dangerous Engagement
Lethal Wedding
Fatal Wedding

Tangled Series
Tangled up in Ice
Tangled up in Pain
Tangled up in Lace
Tangled up in Hate
Tangled up in Love

Black Series
Black Edge
Black Rules
Black Bounds
Black Contract
Black Limit

Not into you Duet

Not into you

Still not into you

Lavish Trilogy

Lavish Lies

Lavish Betrayal

Lavish Obsession

Standalone Novels

Dressing Mr. Dalton

Debt

Offer

Unknown

I owe him a debt. The kind money can't repay.

He wants something else: **me, for one year.**
But I don't even know who he is…

365 days and nights doing everything he wants…except *that*.

"I'm not going to sleep with you," I say categorically.

He laughs.

"I'm going to make you a promise," his eyes challenge mine. **"Before our time is up, you'll beg me for it."**

WHEN THE CHECK ARRIVES...

"What are you doing with that thing?" my roommate, Sydney, asks, walking by my room.

I'm sitting on my bed with my hand wrapped around my knees staring at the envelope that came in the mail a few days ago. My name and address are handwritten in careful capital script and it doesn't have a return address.

I showed it to her when it first arrived and she made fun of me for wanting to actually deposit that *ridiculous* check, her words not mine.

"I was thinking that this person must've dropped it off in our mailbox directly because there's not even a stamp from the post office on this thing," I point out.

Sydney shakes her head and walks out of my sightline for a moment to change into her sweats. When I walk out into our living room, I see her boots neatly put away right next to mine in the foyer. The rain droplets skid off her coat and onto the floor where they make a little puddle, which she quickly cleans up.

I met Sydney Catalano at Wellesley College, but we didn't get really close until our second semester of senior year. She was a double major in biology and chemistry and we met in a required anthropology class that we both put off until we couldn't put it off anymore.

I don't know if it's the case with all biology majors, but Sydney is a very neat and meticulous person who always cleans up after herself, and often after me as well. Though I'm not much of a housekeeper, I take out the garbage and kill spiders to try to be a good roommate.

I pull out last night's Vietnamese takeout from the fridge and warm it up on the stove. We each pile as much as we want onto the plates, leaving the rest on the skillet, before sitting down to eat together around the kitchen island.

"So...what are you going to do?" she asks, tying up her silky black hair in a loose bun while inhaling her food.

My eyes meander over to the envelope, lying flat in between our two plates. Sydney reaches over her food and pulls out the check.

"Olive, this is a joke, okay? This isn't real," she says with a full mouth.

I stare at the numbers in the square box. They are written in the same block script as my address on the envelope.

$167,699.

The amount is written out right under my name and signed with an illegible signature. There is no identifying information anywhere else on the check to give me a glimpse into who it might be from.

"But what if it is?" I ask.

"Why would someone send you a check for this amount and not say who it is or why they're giving you this money?" she asks.

I shrug my shoulders. Of course, I don't have an answer.

"The thing is... I looked up the total amount of my student loans today at work," I say, taking a sip of my water.

"Okay." Sydney nods.

I put down my fork and turn my body toward her.

"What?" She rolls her eyes. "C'mon, the suspense is killing me."

I shake my head. "No, never mind. It doesn't matter," I say, getting up.

She pleads for me to go on and explain but I just take my plate to the sink and wash it. If she thinks that this whole thing is a joke then I don't have to tell her a thing.

"Olive, I'm sorry." Sydney puts her hand on my shoulder. "I don't mean to *not* be supportive. I just don't want you to get hurt. Or in trouble."

I hold up the check to her face.

"You see this number?" I ask, pointing to the amount. She nods. "This is the exact amount that I owe. Down to the penny."

The words surprise her. She exhales slowly and takes a step away from me.

"Really?" she whispers under her breath, taking the check and looking at it more closely.

I nod.

"I had to make a payment today so I looked up the amount, just for the hell of it. Just to make myself feel a little worse about everything," I joke. "But then, the total looked familiar. I realized that I'd seen these numbers somewhere before. I just wasn't sure where. Then when I got home, I saw the envelope on my desk and...there it was. The *exact* amount that I owe in student loans."

Sydney sits back down, stunned by my revelation. I've had about an hour to process this but I'm no less astonished.

"The check arrived a few days ago. So, after you make this payment, you'll owe a little less, right?"

I nod, not sure as to where she is going with this.

"Most of it is going to interest, but yeah, I guess it will be a little less. But the check arrived before this payment was officially due. So, when it came, this is the exact amount of my debt."

We spend the evening talking about the possibilities of what I should do, which basically boil down into two camps.

One, I tear up the check and forget all about it.

Two, I deposit the money, or at least try to.

There is the very real possibility that the check is a fake or some sort of fraud, though whom it is defrauding I have no idea. Still, depositing it is definitely a risk.

"There's something else you should consider," Sydney says. "What happens if you deposit the check and it is real?"

2

WHEN I MAKE A DECISION...

I stare at her for a moment trying to figure out what exactly would be the problem with that situation.

"Why would someone do this? Why would they just give you this gift out of the blue?" she asks.

"I have no idea. I'm still convinced that it's a fake," I say nonchalantly.

"And that's why you want to deposit it?" she asks, calling my bluff.

"Okay, I have no idea. If it's real and it's a gift...I have no idea who has this kind of money or why they would rain it on me."

"We are operating from the position that if this is real, it must be a gift," Sydney says, narrowing her eyes. "But what if it's not a present at all?"

"What do you mean?"

"What if it's just replacing one debt with another? What if this person wants something from you? Wants you to do something for them?"

I take a deep breath. I try to think of all the possibilities of what someone could want from me. The only thing that comes to mind is my job.

"You're a content specialist at a big company," Sydney says, always staying a few steps ahead of me. "What if this is some sort of corporate sabotage?"

I consider that for a moment, but quickly dismiss it. "I don't have any access to anything," I say. "I don't do anything with data or anything that anyone would be interested in."

"I guess," Sydney agrees. "Except that you might be the perfect person to do favors for them from the inside."

Now, it's my turn to roll my eyes. Sydney is someone who spends sixty hours a day cooped in a lab running tissue samples and the rest of the time watching way too many crime and investigation shows.

A few days ago, I applied for a raise and that application required me to submit an updated resume. As a result, I updated my resume and job responsibilities to include *'determining item selection and design for interim formative assessments; writing, reviewing, and revising items aligned to standards including traditional and innovative item types; developing analysis and scoring guides for schools; researching and analyzing items released by the assessment consortia.'*

But what does this all really mean?

"I write math test questions for an educational company," I say. "This check has nothing to do with my job."

"Okay, fine," Sydney concedes, but not really. She just shrugs her shoulders and gives up, leaving behind a seedling of doubt.

What if she's right?

Why would someone send me this check?

What if this does have something to do with my job? And if so, what?

"I'm not agreeing to anything by depositing this check. There's nothing in the memo line. They can't make me do anything illegal," I say.

"Yes, technically, they can't," Sydney agrees. "But people who have this much money to send to strangers...they may not be the most upstanding of citizens."

"So, what do I do?" I ask, staring at the check. "What would you do?"

"I don't know, but then again, I don't owe as much as you do."

"You don't owe anything," I correct her.

Sydney's mother is from a wealthy Chinese family and they had no issues paying fifty thousand dollars a year for her tuition and room and board. I, on the other hand, wasn't as lucky. Despite majoring in mathematics, the best job I could find was this content specialist position that pays fifty-four thousand dollars a year.

Given that Boston is not the cheapest place in the world to live and that our rent is twenty-five hundred a month plus utilities, I will probably be in my fifties before I pay off all of my student debt.

I stare at the amount on the check: one hundred sixty-seven thousand six hundred ninety-nine dollars.

What would paying off this amount mean to my life going forward? Besides having an extra twelve hundred dollars a month as spending money, it would also mean freedom.

My job isn't particularly interesting or challenging and I'd love to try myself in a data analyst position at a start-up or one of the new innovative companies that are popping up around town.

But those companies pay considerably less without providing any healthcare benefits. They do offer stock options, but those stock options are a risk. Not all companies end up being successful in the end. Taking one of those positions is not a risk I could afford to take...before this check arrived.

When I catch my thoughts drifting away from me, I force myself to focus.

Olive, stop it, I say silently to myself. You can't let yourself think about all of that since you don't even know if the check is real.

"There's another possibility," I say to Sydney as she flips on the TV for some mindless distraction. "This whole thing could just be someone's idea of a joke."

"What do you mean?" she says, sitting up.

"Maybe someone is just fucking with me, Like those YouTube videos where someone sets up their friend with a fake winning lottery ticket. The friend gets really excited and then they tell them that it was just a big joke."

"Shit," Sydney says under her breath.

"Yeah...you wouldn't do that to me, would you?" I ask.

"Of course not!"

"Well, I have no idea who would."

"Someone at your office?"

My mind runs over all of the possibilities. We all work in cubicles with very little interaction throughout the day. We're not friends. I hardly know their names. I have no idea why one of them would do this to me.

"I'm going to deposit it," I say, picking up my phone.

"Now?" she gasps.

I open the mobile banking app, taking a picture of the check. I hold my breath and wait for the scan to go through.

A pop-up appears.

"What happened?" Sydney asks, looking over my shoulder.

"The mobile check deposit limit is twenty-five hundred dollars," I read the words on the screen. "I guess I'll have to go into the actual bank."

3

WHEN I GO TO THE BANK...

I hardly sleep a wink that night, tossing and turning until it is dawn. The local branch on the way to my office doesn't open until nine and I have to be at work at 8:30. I walk past their front door, knowing that I have to wait until 10:30 for my break. I'm not an hourly employee so I don't have an official break but that's usually when Marie, my direct superior, goes to the Starbucks across the street for her morning latte. It's a good time to run a short errand.

"Want me to get you anything?" she asks as we ride down the elevator together.

"No, thanks," I say. My mouth runs dry and I cough in the middle of the phrase.

I bury my face in my phone as soon as we get outside, pretending to be very busy with something very important. But what I'm really doing is waiting for her to disappear around the corner so I can head toward the bank in the other direction.

I could've easily told her where I'm heading. Depositing money is a normal errand that people run. What is *not* normal is depositing almost one hundred and sixty-eight thousand dollars in the form of a check from a total stranger.

When I walk up to the teller, my body is visibly shaking. She even comments on it but thinks it has something to do with the cold spell that just blew in from Canada.

"This has been quite a long winter, huh?" the teller asks.

She's dressed in a black business suit and her hair is pulled out of her face. There's a little hole in her nose where a piercing once lived. As she takes my identification, she moves her neck and I spot the tentacles of a large tattoo. It's hard to know what it is exactly, but she quickly adjusts her collar when she catches me staring.

"I'm sorry...it just looks like a pretty awesome tattoo," I say. Her face immediately lights up with a smile.

"It's an octopus wrapped around a large rose bush," she says under her breath. "So what can I do for you?"

My heart sinks.

Okay.

Here it is.

The moment of truth.

I pull out the envelope from my purse and take out the check. I glance at it one last time, bidding it farewell.

Is it illegal to deposit a fake check if you don't know if it's a fake check? A big knot forms in the back of my throat. Perhaps this is something I should've researched before I showed up here. What *if* it is illegal?

"Ma'am?" the teller asks, reaching her hand through the small opening and grabbing the check. When she pulls on it, I have no choice but to let it go.

I search her face for any sign of wrongdoing. Shouldn't she be impressed by the sum? Shocked even? She has access to my account and this amount is definitely not my normal deposit. But her face remains flat and completely without affect.

"Excuse me, I'll be right back," she says and walks away quickly.

Oh my God.

This is it.

She's calling the police.

I should run.

Turn around and go now!

Now!

No, I can't.

I gave her my driver's license and my bank card. What would be the point of running now? They have my address, they'll just come and arrest me there.

The teller comes back with the manager, who has a big smile plastered on his face.

He asks me if I will be taking out any money today and I say no.

At least, I think that's what I say.

I can barely hear myself think over the pounding of blood in between my ears.

"Thank you very much for your

business, Olivia Kernes. Your deposit should be in your account in a few days," the manager says. "Can I help you with anything else?"

His words barely register, but I do manage to shake my head and walk away.

When I get outside, a gust of cold wind collides into me and clears my head. What the hell just happened? They took the deposit. It passed whatever preliminary checks they have.

Of course, that does not mean that I am in the clear. The funds are not released yet and they will not clear and show up in my account for a few days.

So, they can still discover that the check is fake and then...what?

Will they come and arrest me? If they don't arrest me then they'll definitely have a chat with me.

But I'll just tell them the truth. They'll have to believe me. Right?

My mind bounces from one thought to another without even a slight pause.

The rest of the day goes by in a blur. When I tell Sydney what I did, she wants to meet up on our lunch break, twenty minutes from each of our jobs, but I don't have the energy. The weight of what I have just done suddenly feels like there are two heavy anchors wrapped around my feet, pulling me down into the abyss.

I want to run back to the bank, apologize, and make amends, but these same anchors are preventing me from doing anything but sitting in my cubicle and waiting for the hours to pass.

The next two days go by just as slowly. I'm thankful that I got a lead last week on the new assessment project. Maybe this way no one will notice that during these three days, I barely manage to write twenty questions a day. It's hard to do diligent work when you're staring at a dead end for your career, and probably your life.

When I get home that evening, I am mildly shocked that the police aren't there waiting for me. Instead, it is Sydney who greets me with a bottle of Pinot Grigio.

"Okay, don't be mad," she says with a big smile on her face. I furrow my eyebrows and brace myself for the worst.

"You remember how you needed me to log into your bank account a few months ago for that thing?" she asks.

I nod.

"Well, I still had your information saved on my laptop."

"Get to the point."

"The check cleared. You are one hundred and sixty-seven thousand dollars richer!"

4

WHEN I'M SURPRISED...

I stare at Sydney unable to believe my ears. I ask her to repeat what she just said and again I don't believe her. Finally, she pulls out her laptop and shows me my account. I've never seen numbers go up that high before. At least, not numbers that represent money.

I let out a piercing squeal and she joins me immediately. We jump up and down as if we are tween girls at our first concert.

"So, what now?" Sydney asks after we calm down to catch our breaths.

"I don't really know." I shrug. "I guess, I'll pay off my loans."

"Just like that?"

"What else should I do? I mean, this is what the money is intended for, right?"

She nods.

"Do you think I should just do it now?" I ask. "I mean, why wait? I got the money, why not just pay it all off?"

Sydney's eyes get big. I crack my knuckles and look down at my shoes. My feet start to move on their own as I pace around the room back and forth. The euphoria that I felt only moments ago settles somewhere in the pit of my stomach, morphing into a knot.

"Well, you did want to pay them off. You could wait a week or two or you could do it now."

I nod. Or I could do something else altogether.

What if I were to take some of it, just a few thousand, and go on a trip somewhere? I haven't been on a proper vacation since spring break of my senior year and that was two years ago. Yes, there have been a few occasional weekend trips to the Jersey shore but with this money I could go somewhere exotic. Paris. Turks and Caicos. Maybe even Hawaii?!

And what's a few thousand dollars from almost one hundred and sixty-eight thousand? I could pay it all back within a few months and be in the free and clear for life.

"What? What's that look mean?" Sydney asks as a small smile forms at the corner of my lips.

When I tell her what I'm thinking, she gives me a knowing nod.

"I'd love to go on a trip with you," she adds. "I really missed you the last time we all went to the Bahamas."

My shoulders slope down. I'm still not entirely over that. Even though I am not particularly close with Sydney's group of friends from school, she did invite me to an amazing trip that they all took a few months ago. Her job doesn't pay much more than mine does, but she's from a rich family and that means that she doesn't have to save and pinch every penny like I do. None of her friends have to either.

While she does pay rent out of her

salary, her family pays for all of those other nice perks that her life has to offer: a lease on the BMW and first class airfare and lodging to exotic locations. She offered to pay for me to go with them, but I was too ashamed to accept.

Or maybe I was just too proud.

In any case, the trip was split six ways and my part would've cost me six months of rent.

Given that I have a car payment for my Toyota Prius and the student loan payments in addition to rent and utilities, there was no way I could afford anything like that.

"You totally deserve to go on an amazing trip, but maybe it's not the wisest decision," she points out.

I nod, with a deep sigh.

"What you should really do is start some sort of business."

I give her a blank stare.

"Okay, hear me out. I mean, I know that you want to do your master's degree in math and everything, and that's nice, but it's not going to make you money in the long term. You'll always have to work for someone, instead of building up something of your own."

"Is that what you would do?" I ask.

She shrugs. "Yeah, it's something I've been thinking about. I enjoy my work at the lab, but now that I've been there for a bit, it's getting to be monotonous. Every day is the same. Plus, I don't see myself ever making any real money."

"And by real money, you mean what exactly?" I ask.

"Fifty, seventy, one hundred grand... a month."

I smile.

Sydney's concept of wealth varies a lot from my own, but I guess that's understandable since she does come from significantly more money than I do.

"Can you seriously tell me that you will be happy doing this job twenty years from now?" she asks.

"I can seriously tell you that I am *not* happy doing this job now," I say. "But businesses take money to start. And I don't have any."

"Well, you sort of do," Sydney says.

"But I don't even know what business I should start." I say. "Besides, they require work, too. And the money isn't guaranteed."

"Yeah, that's true," she says. "I'm not trying to tell you what to do—"

"Yeah, you kind of are," I point out, smiling.

"Okay, yes, maybe I am. Or maybe I'm just trying to live a little vicariously through you."

"That would be a first." I start to laugh.

Sydney's expression gets serious and she looks away from me twirling a strand of her hair.

"I guess I'm just imagining what I would do with that kind of cash," she says, staring out into space.

"What would you do?" I ask.

5

WHEN I DO IT...

S ydney has an answer for me without missing a beat.

"What would I do?" she asks. "I'd like to start a lifestyle brand. Cute clothes, accessories, bags. Everything organic, cotton, or bamboo. Eco-friendly. Something that looks good on all sizes and women could wear it at all times. Clothes to live in, you know?"

Sydney has always been somewhat of a fashion icon around campus. But recently, her personal style has really evolved to casual wear.

It might have something to do with the fact that she doesn't have to wear a suit to work or it might have something to do with her discovery of dressy leggings that feel like yoga pants. She has a number of pairs from different companies, all of which she has spent days trying to improve upon.

"If that's something you are really interested in, why not?" I ask.

"I've actually done quite a bit of research on it and it shouldn't cost me very much to start it. I'm thinking of investing about thirty-thousand dollars into the whole thing. Spending about six on developing the products and the rest on warehouse fees and shipping, website design, that kind of thing."

"That's awesome," I say. "But you can't have any of my money."

I say it in a joking manner, but I mean every bit of it.

"I don't need your money," she says with a laugh.

I know that that's one hundred percent true.

Her parents give her a modest (her word, not mine) allowance every month, so all she'll have to do is limit some of her expenses for a bit and she'll have her start-up money.

While she talks, I make a decision.

"Okay, I'm going to do it," I say, taking a deep breath.

Sydney focuses her attention on me and waits with anticipation. I grab my laptop and pull out one of the bar stools around our kitchen island.

My fingers immediately turn to ice and I can barely feel the tips hitting the keys. Once I log into the main account, I stare at the amount at the bottom.

I pull the cursor over the Pay Now button.

Once I click that, the site takes me to the page where I have to put in the amount I want to pay. The amount due is nine hundred ninety-seven dollars and forty-nine cents but the total amount on this site is twenty-three thousand five hundred eighty-nine dollars.

"I'm going to do it," I say and type in the full amount.

Once I press send, I'm taken to the confirmation page.

Thank you for paying twenty-three thousand five hundred eighty-nine dollars.

JUST LIKE THAT, I'm almost twenty-four thousand dollars poorer.

My soul is almost twenty-four thousand dollars lighter.

"I thought you owed a lot more than that," Sydney says.

"I do, that's just one of the loan servicing companies that owns my loans," I explain, clicking over to the next one. "By the way, last year some company bought my loans from another company but didn't even bother to contact me or tell me because, according to them, it's my responsibility to somehow know this information. I didn't find out until after a collection agency called me."

"Shit," Sydney says under her breath.

"Yeah, this whole thing is shit," I concur.

The second company gets a payment of

seventy-six thousand two hundred seventy-six dollars.

"One more." I click over to the last account.

"This is so exciting," Sydney says, smiling. "I'm sure they'll be happy to get all these loans paid."

"I think they'll be disappointed that I won't be paying them six percent interest for thirty years. Can you imagine how much they'll lose over the lifetime of the loan?"

I pause before making the last payment.

I stare at the big Pay Now button and imagine the trip that I could take with just a small percentage of this money instead.

Or maybe I could just put some of it into savings, for a rainy day?

These would all be amazing things to do with the extra money, but there's one thing that I probably should do instead: help my mother with her medical bills.

She's had back pain for a number of years and the surgery seemed to have made things worse. She has to pay over twelve hundred dollars a month just to maintain her medical insurance and there's still a big copay for her monthly medications and doctor visits. In addition, she owes about thirty-thousand for her portion of the surgery expenses.

I don't like to think about this much, and I talk about it even less. Sydney knows the broad strokes of my mother's medical condition but not the stress that comes with not knowing how you're going to pay for all of these expenses without losing your apartment.

Maybe I should use the money to help her? But the thing about medical expenses is that more and more of them come every month. If I were to pay off my student loans then I would be free of them forever.

I type in the numbers one by one.

6..7...8...3...4

I place the cursor over the Pay Now button and press it without another hesitation. A confirmation page appears.

Thank you for paying sixty-seven thousand eight hundred thirty-four dollars.

I let out a big sigh of relief. Sydney

grabs me by my shoulders and gives me a big hug.

She wants to jump up and down but I don't have the energy.

I feel like all of the wind has been knocked out of me.

I'm in shock by what I've done.

Stunned.

It is only later that night, when I'm lying alone in my room, that tears start to flow down my face. My whole body starts to shake uncontrollably.

I wrap myself in my comforter and get into the fetal position to weather the attack.

The tears are hot and salty. My eyes burn as does the small cut that I had on the inside of my lip.

After some time, the flow slows down. Suddenly I am able to catch my breath and a few moments later, I wipe my cheeks for the last time.

It is only then that I realize that these weren't tears of sorrow, but rather tears of joy and relief. Whatever may or may not happen in the future, at least this part of my life is over. This debt that has been weighing so heavily on me, making me feel like I'm drowning, it's gone.

Vanished.

Vanquished.

Erased.

And now, I'm free.

6

WHEN I GET AN INVITATION...

The following week goes by in a blur. My mother has one of her pain episodes and I spend two nights at her house helping her out and making sure that she has everything she needs. Whenever her back acts up, her mind always goes to a dark ugly place and she starts to blame my father for everything that went wrong in her life. If my father hadn't gotten her pregnant at eighteen then their strict parents would've never forced them to marry. If they had never gotten married then she wouldn't have spent her life taking care of him.

"I had dreams, you know, I wasn't

always this fat and ugly," she says, lying in her bed, watching television while holding her iPad in her hand.

She doesn't care what I have to say or how this makes me feel, she just needs me to be here to listen. So, that's what I do.

"But it's having you kids that made me this way. It's having your good for nothing alcoholic father that made me eat everything in sight. Do you know what it feels like to have your husband spend every paycheck at the bar, leaving me alone to take care of you brats. On what money? I had to beg the next door neighbor to lend me some so I could buy you milk."

I want to roll my eyes, but I resist the temptation. It's not that I'm not sympathetic to everything she has been through, it's just that I've heard this series of stories over and over again all of my life.

"Patrick," she says, looking wistfully at the window. "If only he had lived, then everything would've been fine."

Yeah, all of our family's troubles would be immediately solved if only my mother's favorite child was still alive.

"He would've married a nice Catholic girl and they would've given me four or five grandkids to be busy with," she continues. "Not like you...or your brother, Owen."

"You can barely take care of yourself," I mumble under my breath.

"What?!" she hisses. "What did you say?" She pulls the iPad away from her as if she's going to swat me with it.

On impulse, from a decade of memories, I cower away from her.

"I wouldn't have any of these issues if Patrick was still here!" she roars.

Usually, I just tune her out and go through what needs to be done. Today is no different. What I want to say is that she can't just blame Dad and Patrick's death on every shitty thing that happened in her life. But this would be adding fuel to her fire.

Patrick, my oldest brother, died on his eighteenth birthday in a car crash. Our father gave him a car and he crashed it into the side of a hill. The police said that they estimated his speed was well over one hundred miles per hour, but Mom doesn't believe a word of that report. She also refuses to believe that he had a high blood alcohol level because he promised her that he would never drink and drive.

She doesn't say anything for a while, letting me fold her laundry in peace. But during the commercial break, she turns to me and asks, "So, what about you?"

"What do you mean?"

"When are you going to give me some grandchildren?"

"Mom, I'm not seeing anyone."

"That hasn't stopped almost every other girl in this neighborhood from toting around a toddler on her hip."

"I don't want a child...right now," I say.

"What does that matter?" she asks, sitting up a bit in bed. Her pain medication must've started working because she's suddenly full of energy. "If people only had children they wanted, the world would be a lot less populated."

I fold a large fitted sheet and put it in the back of the closet with the rest.

"I mean, it's not like Owen can give me any grandkids at this point," she says. "So I guess I'll have to settle for yours."

Owen is doing ten years in the state penitentiary for an armed robbery charge.

"He may get parole," I point out.

"Yeah, right!"

"I have years to have kids and so does Owen. I'm sure that you'll get some grandkids in the future," I say to make nice.

Mom sits up a bit, narrowing her eyes. Her hair is stringy and unkempt and she's dressed in her usual long puffy nightgown that she wears day and night. Her face is splotchy and looks much older than her forty-eight years.

"Are you stupid or something? Why did you waste all of that money on education if you're still as dense as you were growing up? Don't you get it? I want *you* to have kids for *me*. I want *Owen* to have kids for *me*. I want some damn grandkids *now*."

I used to think that she looked older than she was because of her hard life, her drinking, and her pain medication. But now I think she looks older because of her meanness.

Luckily, the commercial ends and her attention goes back to her program. I head into the kitchen to make lunch, but then sneak out onto the back porch for some fresh air.

The trees are only now starting to bud and the weather is still cold and unwelcoming. But the cold feels good on my face.

When I first paid off my loans, I wasn't sure if it was the right decision. My mother has a lot of medical bills and perhaps I should've used some of the money to help her. But the last two days told me that I did the right thing.

Paying off my mom's bills wouldn't have improved her situation that much and she wouldn't have even appreciated it if I had.

Zipping up my coat, I slip my hands into the pockets. Feeling the outline of the envelope that arrived yesterday sends shivers up my spine. The paper is thick and luxurious and the letter itself has gold foil around the border.

I pull it out and look at it again. I run my fingers over the insignia at the top. There are no floral leaves or lions standing on their back legs, but it is no less elegant and exquisite: a large C enclosed in a box.

Dear Ms. Olivia E. Kernes, I begin to read the words again silently, but moving my lips.

7

WHEN I READ THE LETTER...

"What the hell are you doing here?" Mom swings open the screen door, hitting me with it in my back. When the meds are working, she doesn't need the cane and instead uses it as a weapon.

I drop the letter onto the floor and quickly scramble to get it.

"What is that?" she asks, pointing her cane at me.

"Nothing, just...bills."

Holding the door open, she waits for me to walk past her and then grabs the letter out of my hand.

"What are you doing?" I reach to get it

back, but she pushes me back with her cane.

"You have always been so secretive. Even when you were just a little kid. Writing stuff in your little diary, putting a lock on it and hiding it under your bed," she says.

Unwilling to physically grab it from her, I stand and wait.

"Dear Ms. Olivia E. Kernes," she starts to read. "Thank you for accepting my gift. I know that you have used it in a meaningful way. What is *this* about?"

I shrug and shake my head.

"I know that you must have questions as to who has sent it to you and why. I would like to alleviate your curiosity and invite you to my home for an introduction. Please know that any and all expenses will be taken care of. I hope to see you there."

I have read this letter so many times since it arrived that I have the words memorized. Below that is the signature line that reads,

Sincerely, NC
Maui, Hawaii

. . .

PS. If you accept my invitation, please email me at nc@apricotway.com

"WHAT THE HELL IS THIS ABOUT?" Mom demands to know. "What gift?"

I'm not sure how to answer this question except I cannot tell her the truth.

First of all, she doesn't know the extent of the loans that I owed because she thought me wanting to get an education was my way of wanting to be better than her.

Second of all, I cannot tell her that I received a check in that amount and didn't share a penny with her.

"I got a gift in the mail. I wasn't sure who it was from, but it was nice and I kept it," I lie.

She narrows her eyes.

Unlike my brother, I'm not a very good liar and she's a very good investigator. One of the things that I did learn from Owen is that the best lies are those that are closest to the truth.

"What is it?" she asks.

I hesitate.

I can't tell her that I got any money because she'll expect me to share it with her. But I do have to tell her something.

"A small statue of an...elephant," I mumble.

A few days ago, I saw this clay elephant at my favorite thrift store and I considered buying it. But it was forty-five dollars and kind of an extravagant expense for a pretty useless object. Now, I make a mental note that I have to go back and get it, if for no other reason than to have it in my possession in case she asks to see it.

"An elephant? Why would someone send that to you?"

"I have no idea."

"And now this NC wants you to go see him?" she asks, pointing to the letter. "Go to Maui, all expenses paid?"

I shrug.

Mom comes so close to me I can smell the stale cigarette smoke on her skin. Her dark eyes look vicious. I take a step back but the hallway is so narrow that my back touches the walls. There's nowhere to go.

"What the hell are you up to, Olive? You trying to find yourself a rich man or something?"

"No, ma'am." I shake my head.

"'Cause you know that you can't. You're too ugly and fat. Why would he want you?"

Her words land as if she was actually punching me.

Tears start to well up in my eyes.

My mouth gets parched and I try to swallow the big ball forming in the back of my throat.

I've heard her say these things to me since I was a little kid so you'd think that I would be used to hearing them by now. But I guess that's the thing about mothers, you only get one and you keep giving her chances because you don't want to lose her.

She takes a step back and pours herself a cup of stale coffee. "You want any?" she asks.

"No, thank you."

"Listen, I don't mean to be hard on you but that's the kind of world we live in. You seem to live in the clouds. You are pretty enough to make someone a wife, but you're not pretty the way those Hollywood actresses are. I just don't want you to be disappointed, honey."

I nod. Her sudden shift in tone and her pretense that she is saying all of this for my benefit makes me feel even worse.

"Listen, I have to go," I say.

"You're not going to stay tonight? What if I need you?"

"You'll be fine. I set up all of your medicine next to your bed, the laundry is done. The food will be here shortly," I say, grabbing my duffel bag and my phone and charger out of the wall.

"Fine, go!" she says coldly.

"Can I have my letter please?"

"No, absolutely not," she says, shaking her head. Then she takes out a cigarette and lights my letter on fire with the lighter.

I don't bother grabbing it out of her hand. Instead, I stand there in a trance watching it burn. The same fate came to my high school diploma the day after I graduated and my first passport when I was foolish enough to have it sent to our house.

"This is for your own good," she says.

"Okay," I say, walking out.

"You're not going to say goodbye?" she yells after me as I close the door behind me.

Tears start to stream down my face before I get inside my car. I can barely see through them as I open the Note app on my phone and type up the letter that I have committed to memory. When I'm finished, I stare at the email address that NC provided.

I don't know who sent this gift or why, but I do know two things. One, I am going to accept this invitation. Two, I am never going to see my mother again.

8

WHEN I GET READY...

"You can't go there by yourself," Sydney says, walking into my room and closing my suitcase. I go into my closet and grab a strapless dress I haven't worn since last summer.

"What do you think about this one?" I ask, pressing it to my body and extending one leg in front of the other. It's very soft and has a light floral design, hanging loosely like a tunic. The neckline is made of a twisted gold material that gives it a bit of flair.

"Olive, you're not thinking clearly. You just spent a few days at your mom's and that always makes you a little crazy."

"I'm not doing this because of her," I say.

"So, why? Why are you doing this?"

I shrug. "I want to know who sent me the money."

"This could be a really dangerous thing, Olive. You could be sex-trafficked for crying out loud."

"I doubt that."

"What makes you so sure?" Sydney asks.

"Sex traffickers don't usually send you over a hundred and fifty grand ahead of time."

"Whatever." She throws up her hands. "You know what I mean. What do you even know about this NC?"

I shrug.

"He has an email address, woohoo!" she says sarcastically. "Apricot Way. Do you know what that is?"

"No, I tried to look it up but I couldn't find anything about it."

"Well, I found out something."

I fold another pair of leggings and look up at her. "What?"

"There are like a hundred people with the acronyms N. C. In Maui."

"I don't doubt it," I say.

Sydney walks up to me and puts her hands around my shoulders.

"What did your mom say to you, Olive?" she asks.

Her lips are trembling and she looks terrified. I've never seen her this concerned about anything before.

Sydney is the one person in my life who knows the most about my mother and what she has put me through. Lately, it seems like all I do is complain to her about what's going on in my life, but she has always been there for me. I appreciate her listening more than she will ever know.

"Nothing special, just the usual shit," I say.

Thankfully, she has never asked me why I put up with all of it. She has her own issues with her parents, mainly the fact that no matter how much she succeeds she never seems to quite live up to their expectations. So, she knows exactly why I put up with all the crap that my mother delves out.

My mom's mean and angry and has never had many friends. The few that remained were driven out of her life over the last year when her pain and her hatred got worse. My father went out for a carton of milk never to return again. One of my brothers is dead and the other is serving a long prison sentence. My mother is all I have and I can't just give up on her. At least, that's what I always told myself to get through it before.

"I'm done," I say quietly.

"What do you mean?"

"I've had enough. She caught me with that letter, she read it, she mocked me, and she lit it on fire."

"I am so sorry," Sydney whispers, putting her arm around me.

"I can't keep letting her treat me like this," I say. "I know that she has a lot of pain, but I have to stop accepting that as an excuse."

"Is that why you're doing this?" she asks. I shrug.

I open my underwear drawer and pick out a few black panties and my favorite t-shirt bra. I decide to pack another significantly less comfortable lacy one as well, just in case a special occasion comes up.

"Yeah, that's partly why I'm doing this. I need to get away. I took a week off work and I figure I'll take my chance on this."

"I know that you want to go somewhere but...I'm just worried that this isn't a safe thing to do," Sydney says.

"I'll have my phone on me. As soon as I get there and I know exactly where I'm going, I'll text you. I promise."

She walks over to my closet and pulls out a red dress. Folding it up carefully, she packs it into my suitcase.

"But this is your favorite dress," I say. It's also one of my favorite ones to borrow.

"I know, but I want you to take it. For good luck." I wrap my arms around Sydney and give her a kiss on the cheek.

We say our goodbyes as I wait for the car to pick me up downstairs.

Once I wrote back to the email address

provided in the letter, Amelia Dual, a concierge, wrote me back immediately with all of the arrangements.

Even though I'm not much of a phone talker, I didn't feel comfortable doing all of this online. So, we video chatted and she explained what will happen.

She will send a car to pick me up at my apartment, which will then take me to Logan International Airport. I received the flight information in my email: a First-Class ticket to Maui, Hawaii, with a brief stop in Los Angeles. Once there, another car will take me to my final destination.

I get to the airport an hour before my flight and wander around the shops, leafing through the magazines and debating what kind of junk food is the healthiest to buy for the plane. I message Amelia about the exact location of where I am going, but she refuses to provide me with any additional details.

An email trail, car service, and first class tickets definitely make me feel safer about the fact that I am probably not being kidnapped.

Still, Sydney's concerns echo my own. The thing is that I don't really know what I'm getting myself into and I'm doing it all alone.

First-class passengers board first and a flight attendant offers me a warm towel and asks for my drink order.

"She'll have a bloody Mary," a familiar voice says, grabbing the empty seat next to mine. "I'll have one, too."

"What are *you* doing here?" I ask.

9

WHEN SHE SURPRISES ME...

Sydney takes the seat next to mine with a mischievous look on her face. She takes her time and builds anticipation with first putting her carry-on luggage in the overhead bin and then unpacking her earbuds, iPad, and phone, putting them into the compartment in the back of the seat in front of her.

Finally, she turns to me and says, "I'm coming with you."

I start to laugh, shaking my head.

A wave of relief sweeps over me.

I hadn't realized until this very moment how much I was dreading doing this on my own.

Sydney is not technically invited, but I don't care. They can't expect me to go out there all alone, not knowing what I am walking into.

"So, you just...what? Booked a ticket yourself?"

"Yep," she says, tossing her shiny hair from her shoulders. "I saw the itinerary and the flight that you were on and I booked mine the same day."

"You're so sweet," I say, squeezing her hand. "It must've cost you a fortune."

"Don't worry, I told my dad that I need some girl time with my roomie and we're getting away for the week."

"You're staying the whole week?"

"I can easily change the tickets if you don't want me to. Don't worry."

THE FLIGHT IS long but uneventful.

I read a book on my phone, I stare into space, I page through the magazines I got at the gift shop back in Boston.

I eat two packets of peanut M&M's even

though I promised myself that I would save them until Hawaii.

I try to sleep but my mind keeps running around in circles so I entertain myself with three movies and consume an enormous amount of pretzels and two packets of salt and vinegar potato chips.

When we arrive and get our bags, we walk up to the man holding a sign with my name on it and follow him to his car.

He has jet black hair with a few wisps of gray, dark olive skin, and a mega-watt smile.

Dressed in a flowing Hawaiian shirt, khaki pants, and leather flip-flops, he looks exactly like what I imagined every man on this island to look like.

"Wow, interesting choice," Sydney says, looking around the new model Jeep Wrangler as Thomas, our driver, loads our bags.

I guess I was expecting a man in a black suit and a Lincoln town car or a BMW because I'm just as surprised by the greeting as she is.

On the drive out, I plaster my face to the

window staring at the lush vegetation on either side of the highway.

"The first explorer to come to Maui was Admiral Jean-Francois de La Perouse in 1786," Thomas, our driver, says.

"It's so beautiful here," I say, looking at bright blue water and the pristine beaches on one side of us.

"Maui is the second largest Hawaiian island with over 120 miles of coastline and beaches. The island itself is over 727 square miles."

"It looks very wild." Sydney points out to the luscious green jungles on the other side of the road.

"It is. Not all roads around here are easily drivable but that's partly what makes it so charming. It has a lot of hidden places. One of which is where you are going."

My ears perk up.

"And where's that?"

"I am under strict instructions not to reveal a thing, I am sorry," Thomas says, quickly changing the subject. "This road, the Hana Highway, is considered one of the most scenic ones in the world."

I look down and watch the way the asphalt looks as if it's almost hugging the cliffs. Sydney, who is terrified of heights, moves closer to the middle of the car and shields her eyes.

The highway doesn't match any normal definition of a highway. There are hundreds and hundreds of breathtaking and hairpin turns that alternate between waterfalls on one side and soaring and plunging sea cliffs on the other.

We drive for nearly two hours then turn onto a poorly paved road that goes through the lush tropical rainforest, so thick that it's just a sea of green. Rain comes and goes, leaving behind a sparkling rainbow.

We drive out onto a clearing, a beautiful green pasture. There are dramatic mountains behind us and miles of a deep blue ocean in the front. The grass moves slightly in the breeze almost as if it were dancing. Were it not for the sprawling home positioned near the cliff, this place would be completely wild.

As we pull up closer to the house, I am surprised by how it looks. Instead of the brand new Mediterranean type of estate that I imagined this would be, this house is a blast from the past.

Thick plantation shutters, a ranch-style design, and a wrap-around lanai gives me a feeling of old Hawaii, the kind that I've only seen in movies. There is extensive ocean frontage with an infinity pool that looks out onto the water below.

Slightly to the back of the house, there are two cottages painted the same soothing taupe color as the main house. They also have matching thick shutters and oscillating ceiling fans on the porches.

My eyes are immediately drawn to something in the distance that is perched almost over the cliff.

"What's that?" I ask.

"That's our gazebo. It's perfect for watching turtles, whales, and other wildlife," Thomas says.

"Can I go take a look?" I ask.

"No, not just yet," he says, getting my suitcases.

"I will show you to your cottage, Ms.

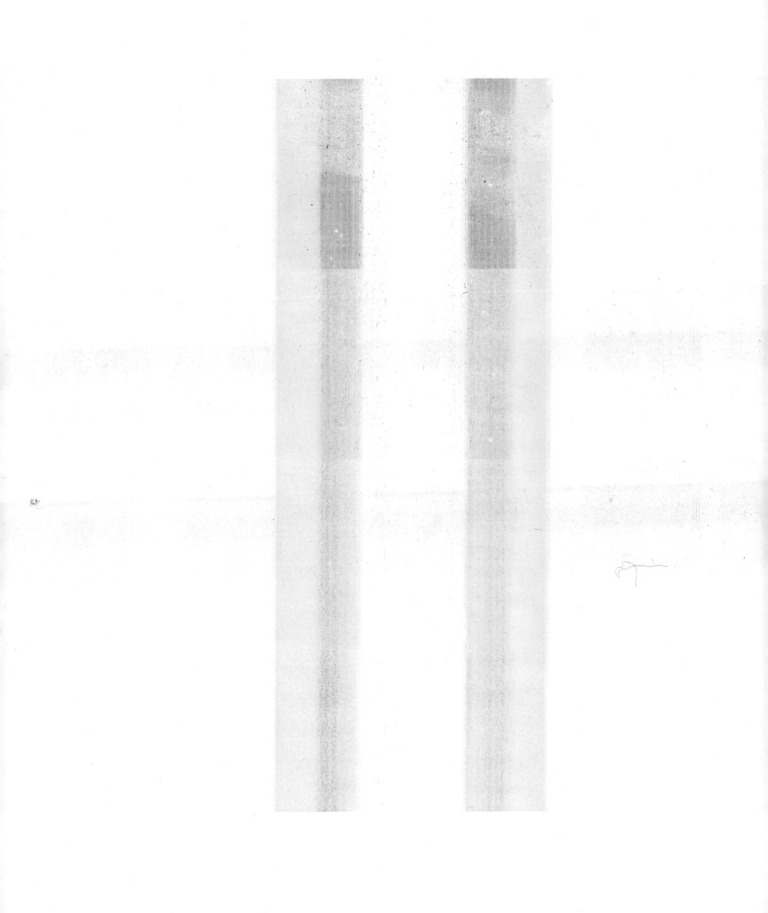

Kernes, and our staff will get the other one ready for you, Ms. Catalano," Thomas says.

I don't know if he's just too polite to say anything about me bringing a friend along, but now suddenly I feel very uncomfortable about Sydney's presence. I am an invited guest, maybe I had no right to invite my roommate along on this trip.

When we follow Thomas to my cottage, a beautiful woman with dark flowing hair and a flower behind her left ear walks up to us. She's dressed in a casual summer dress and wedges and gives me a warm hug.

"It's so nice to meet you, Ms. Kernes," she says. "I'm Amelia Dual."

10

WHILE WE WAIT...

Amelia shows us my cottage. It's a spacious one-bedroom with comfortable off-white furniture and a beautiful marble kitchen island. A large television hangs above the fireplace. I'm immediately drawn to the floor-to-ceiling sliding doors that span the whole side of the place, looking out onto the ocean below. Large palm trees cradle the place on either side, putting me strangely at ease at being here.

"Mr. Crawford hopes that you will be comfortable here, Ms. Kernes," Amelia says.

"Please call me Olive," I correct her. "And she's Sydney."

"Yes, of course," Amelia says. "Would you mind waiting here, Sydney, while I get someone to set up your cottage?"

"Of course, no problem." She nods.

Amelia is also too nice to say anything, but I feel like I have to.

"Sydney can stay with me, it's no problem," I say. "I'm sorry that I didn't tell you about this earlier but...I was unsure about coming here all by myself since I don't know why I was even invited here."

"You don't have to apologize. You are our guest and Mr. Crawford will understand," she says and leaves.

Sydney and I exchange looks. She doesn't have to say a word, I know exactly what she's thinking by the expression on her face. She thinks this place is amazing and is very impressed with the professionalism of the staff.

There's a plate of fruit and pastries sitting on the edge of the kitchen counter along with a collection of teas, some of which are Hawaiian. I forgo the traditional ones like Earl Grey and peppermint and steep a bag of the local mango, pineapple, and passion fruit. Sydney makes herself a cup of Royal Kona coffee and takes the tray of food out onto the lanai overlooking the sea.

"So, what do you think?" she asks, taking a sip.

My mouth salivates at the sight of the slices of bright yellow starfruit and I quickly bite into one.

"I don't know what to think," I say. "I mean, why am I here? Who brought me here?"

"Apparently, Mr. Crawford did," Sydney says, her eyes lighting up. "Do you know of any Mr. Crawford?"

I shake my head no.

"Think hard. Do you know of anyone with the last name Crawford at all?"

I think about it for a moment. But the answer is again no.

"I don't remember anyone named Crawford growing up. I don't remember even meeting a Crawford before."

We sit out on the porch enjoying the

light breeze and watching the whitecaps of the ocean below collide with the pristine white beach. The flight was long and tiring, and I can't help but sit back in my rocking chair and close my eyes. I listen to the chirping of birds somewhere in the distance until I fall into a deep sleep.

"She's coming back," Sydney whispers to me, rousing me.

I don't know how much time has passed but there are three fewer croissants than there were before I fell asleep.

Amelia walks up to us and tells us that Sydney's cottage is now ready.

Sydney insists on carrying her own bags so I just follow her down a footpath to her place, which is identical to mine in every way down to the nautical decorations and throw pillows.

"Mr. Crawford is hosting a cocktail party tonight at six at the main house. He would like to invite you both there," Amelia says.

"Yes, of course," I mumble, rubbing my eyes.

"It's only three now, so if you want to take a rest or a dip in the pool, feel free," she says. "There are towels and bathing suits and anything else you may need in your cottages."

After Amelia leaves, Sydney says she's going to take a nap but I want to go on a walk to clear my head. I'm afraid that going to sleep now is just going to make me more drowsy for the party. Hey, maybe I'll even do a few laps in the pool.

I change out of my sweaty leggings and black t-shirt and into a light sleeveless beach dress. It's unfitted and airy, like a long t-shirt, and finally I enjoy the way the breeze feels wrapping around my bare legs as I make my way toward the cliff.

"There must be some way down," I say to myself, looking down at the ocean below. I'm standing at the edge of a nearly twenty-foot cliff.

I walk over to the batch of swaying palm trees to one side and examine the rugged terrain again. The overhang back toward the main house is a near straight up and down face, but there does seem to be more of a path in the direction toward the rainforest.

I head in there and then slowly start to make my way down the narrow winding trail down the rocky bluff.

This walk is no joke and I'm about halfway down before I realize that this may have been a really bad decision.

With each step, I kick up the sand and rocks and a few fall straight down below. Each time I place my feet onto the ground, I test it first to make sure that it's stable but one time I'm wrong. My foot slips and I land on my butt and start to slide all the way to the bottom.

"Are you okay?" A guy runs over to me.

Putting down his surfboard, he kneels down next to me and we both stare at my bleeding leg. I move it around to assess the damage.

"It seems to be okay," I say. "Just a few cuts and bruises."

"Did you just come down this way?" he asks, pointing to the precipice above. The trail that I thought was a path doesn't look anything like it from this direction and I'm kind of shocked that I even made it all of the way down without breaking my back.

"I wanted to touch the water," I say, getting up and straightening my dress.

"Well, if you want to go back up, make sure to go that way." He points a little further down the beach. "That's where the real trail starts."

I'm about to ask him for his name, but he dives into the water before I can get the chance.

"Thanks!" I yell after him. He raises his hand for an acknowledgment and disappears below the waves.

11

WHEN WE GET READY...

I can't help but wade in the water and swim around a bit. I would go skinny dipping, but the surfer is still somewhere on the horizon so I go in with my dress on.

When I get to my cottage, I hang up my dress and jump straight into the shower. Fresh water feels good on my scrapes as the tingling from the salt finally goes away.

When I examine my legs closer, I see the scratches from the rocks go almost the whole way down from my thighs to my ankles. The bleeding has stopped, but after the hot shower, the scrapes look pretty bad.

Wrapped in a towel, I go through my suitcase trying to figure out what to wear to this cocktail party. I have no idea how dressy or not dressy it is and I'm always a little uncomfortable in being overdressed. Unlike Sydney, I'd rather be the girl that few people notice.

I'm ready half an hour ahead of schedule and go to see Sydney who is probably still in the midst of her transformation. She lets me in with her hair still wet and a tornado of clothes on her bed.

"Is that what you're wearing?" she gasps.

I smile from getting the reaction that every girl dreams of when she takes the time to get a look together.

"What's wrong with this?" I ask.

"Jeans? Really?"

"They aren't jeans, they are black jean leggings and they make my butt and legs look really nice," I say.

Paired with a pair of nude wedges and a flowing, sleeveless top with a plunging neckline, I know that I look sophisticated but not overdressed.

"And what if this is some sort of black tie thing?"

"It's a cocktail party, I'm wearing cocktail attire. C'mon, you're the one who always says that a nice pair of heels dresses up any outfit."

"Yeah, I know," she says loudly over the sound of the hairdryer. "I just thought you'd wear my dress."

I shrug. I'd given that a thought as well, but I couldn't. I don't know what I'm walking into here and I need to feel as comfortable as possible. I'm not good at heels and dresses in general, and I'm only willing to sacrifice one of those tonight. Sydney knows all of this, of course, so she doesn't push me any further.

Even though it doesn't look like she would have enough time to do everything that she needs to get done for her to look presentable, Sydney is ready by exactly six o'clock. It's amazing how quickly she dries and straight irons her hair, applies her makeup, and slips on her little black dress.

"I figured that I'd go with the classic

cocktail look," she says, applying one last coat of red lipstick to complete the look.

"You look beautiful," I say.

"As do you." She gives me a quick squeeze on the hand. "I'm sorry if I made you feel bad earlier, I was just joking."

"I know you were." I smile back at her.

THE SUN IS JUST STARTING to set and the wrap-around lanai is illuminated with a brilliant explosion of pinks, yellows, and reds. Waiters, dressed in black tuxes, meander among the guests who are dressed in almost casual attire with men wearing Hawaiian shirts and khakis and women floral dresses. Some are sleeveless, others are strapless, and wrap-style but all move softly in the light breeze coming off the ocean.

I don't have the skills to be able to walk up to a perfect stranger and start a conversation, but luckily Sydney does. Within a few moments, I am engrossed in a discussion about Boston with a couple of

women in their thirties who have never
been there.

They both grew up in Hawaii, on
different islands, and now work in real
estate. If it were up to me, I would just keep
talking to them all night, but Sydney has an
effortless way of flowing in and out of
conversations and quickly we move on to
new people. Within the hour, we have
talked to almost half of the attendees.

There are a few commonalities among
them. Most are in their thirties and forties
and live on Maui. Many of the women do
not work and those who do, work in real
estate. The men are involved in various
investment projects 'on the island,' that's
what they say when referring to this place.

In every conversation, I keep meaning
to ask about Mr. Crawford, but then I
always get a little bit shy. I don't really want
to go into the reason why I'm here and I
fear that if they find out that I don't even
know who he is then I will inevitably
have to.

As Sydney leads us to yet another group
of strangers for another round of small talk,

I look around for Amelia or Thomas, the only familiar faces who know him. I spot Amelia inside, by the grand piano. The party seems to congregate outside, with barely anyone inside the main living area. I pull away from Sydney and follow a waiter through the sliding glass doors.

"Hey!" I yell to her from across the room. I'm so eager to speak to her that I barely notice the cathedral ceilings, the minimalist furniture, and the expansive view of the water.

Amelia meets up with me by the stone fireplace.

"Are you having a good time?" she asks. "Oh, you don't have a drink!"

"No, I'm good," I say, realizing that I left mine on one of the tables outside.

Despite my protestations, she flags down one of the waiters and I take a glass of white wine off his serving tray. I'm not much of a drinker, but not having a glass in your hand at a cocktail party, even if it's just water, seems off-putting.

"I just wanted to ask you about Mr. Crawford," I say, with hesitation in my voice. "I don't know if I was supposed to meet him out there or ...not."

"No, he actually just got delayed with a business meeting so he is running quite a bit late," Amelia says. "He told me to tell you that he hopes that you are enjoying the party and your stay here and he will see you later."

I nod, as if I understand a word of what she is saying. Then I decide to just come out with it.

"Okay," I say slowly, carefully picking my words. "Can I ask you something?"

"Sure." She shrugs her shoulders in a casual nonchalant manner as if she has not a care in the world.

"Who is *he*?" I blurt out.

"Who is Mr. Crawford?" she asks, surprised.

12

WHEN I WAIT...

"Yes, who is he? What does he look like? Do I know him from somewhere?" I ask Amelia. The words burst out of my mouth, all at once.

Suddenly, Amelia's demeanor changes completely. The smile on her face vanishes and she shakes her head.

"Do you know why I'm here? I mean, do you know what he did for me?"

"I know that he sent you a gift and he was thankful that you accepted it," she says coolly. "Actually, I was the one who took care of the arrangements."

"Yes, I figured that much," I say. I wait for her to continue but she doesn't. Instead, she just stares at me like a deer in headlights.

"So...can you tell me anything about him?" I nudge her again.

"No, I'm sorry. I really can't." She shakes her head. "He gave me strict instructions to not reveal anything to you about who he is."

"Do you know why he sent me the gift?"

"That I actually do *not* know."

At a loss as to what to do next, I look back at the party on the deck.

"Does anyone there know who he is?" I ask.

She hesitates. Her eyes drift down to the floor and then cautiously back to me.

"Please tell me," I plead.

"They are just his friends and business associates, but he likes to keep his private life private."

My eyes light up.

"Olive, please." Amelia touches my hand. The expression on her face is intense and serious. "Please don't ask them. Mr. Crawford doesn't want the surprise spoiled and none of them know what he did for you. It is his wish to keep that a secret."

Her eyes meet mine and she doesn't let me go even when I take a step away from her.

"Please, promise me that you'll wait," she says.

I don't know what the right thing to do is so I nod and give her my word. If that's what he wants, then that's the least I can do in return for him giving me such an extraordinary gift.

I spend the rest of the evening avoiding all the people that I have met earlier. I figured that I have done enough socializing for one party and now that the illusive Mr. Crawford isn't making an appearance, I'd rather just enjoy this view in peace.

When the night comes to a close and the sky becomes spotted with millions of stars, Sydney runs up to me in a huff. She's so excited that it takes her a moment to catch her breath.

"I have a date!" she finally manages to say.

"Really? With who?" I ask.

"This guy I met at the party. He is tall and has this amazing luscious dark hair and a beautiful tan."

"Everyone around here has a beautiful tan," I point out.

"Whatever." She waves her hand. "He's also a doctor!"

"Oh, a doctor! Your parents will be so proud," I joke.

"No, they won't," she says proudly. "He's a pediatrician at this clinic for the poor. If he has money it doesn't come from his job."

"Oh, I see, he's a medical rebel!" I say, smiling. "So...where is he taking you?"

"To dinner and a drive," she says. "Don't wait up."

I feel the expression on my face fall. "You're leaving now?"

"Yeah, why do you care?"

I shrug.

I shouldn't.

I should be happy for her, but I'm concerned nevertheless.

"But you just met him, what if he's some...creep or something?"

"He's not! Besides, how is this any

different from me meeting some doctor at a party in Boston?"

I shake my head. "Well, neither of us have ever been here before, for one. What if you get in trouble? You don't know the area at all."

"I'll have my phone with me."

"There's no reception here on that main road, remember?" My thoughts return to our two hour drive.

During daylight, it was magnificent but the fact that I couldn't get a signal at all was a little bit annoying. Now, that it's nighttime, the road seems treacherous and dangerous.

"I'll be fine," Sydney says and I let it go. I don't want to ruin her night by acting like her mother, or worse, but I still have my concerns.

"Look, it's going to be fine. Amelia knows him. It's not like he's a total stranger. Besides, you're the one you should be worried about."

"What do you mean?" I ask.

"Mr. Crawford? Wasn't he supposed to be at the party? And he's a no-show?"

She laughs, tossing her hair off her shoulders.

"Maybe he was traveling here on that crazy road, fell off a cliff, and doesn't have reception to call for help," I joke, and then immediately regret it.

That seems like something that probably happens a lot around here and I feel bad for even kidding about it.

"So, what is going on with the elusive Mr. Crawford?" she asks as I follow her back to her cottage.

"I don't know. Amelia said that he got held up with something but who knows if that's true. She was being very cryptic about everything and asked me not to ask the guests about his whereabouts."

"How odd," Sydney agrees.

She walks into the bathroom and applies a fresh coat of deodorant to her underarms. Then she props up her leg on the sink to check if she needs to shave them again. The knees and the area around the ankle of her left leg don't pass inspection so she gets out her razor and shaves those hairs off.

The doorbell rings. Sydney's eyes light up in excitement. She practically runs over, but then takes a moment to gather her thoughts prior to opening the door.

The man on the other side is indeed tall, dark, and very handsome. He gives her a brief peck on the cheek and then introduces himself to me as James Dupree.

"Please don't take this the wrong way, but can I have the name of the restaurant where you are going and your phone number and address? Just in case," I say.

I'm rarely this forward but I know that I will regret not having this information were she to spend the night with him.

He smiles and asks for my number so that he can text me all the info.

"I'm sorry but we're just not from around here and I wouldn't want anything to happen to Sydney," I say as he types his message.

"No offense taken, you're being a good friend," he says. "Just sent it."

I follow them out of her cottage and head toward my own.

"Wait, James!" I yell into the dark. I

follow the path toward the two figures somewhere in the distance. "Can I ask you something?"

They're holding hands and Sydney has an annoyed expression on her face.

"I just wanted to ask you about the guy who owns that house. I don't know if Sydney told you anything about why we're here..." My words trail off.

"No, not really," James says.

I hear Amelia's request in my mind and hesitate to tell him anything else.

"So, do you know the owner?" I reiterate the question.

"Nicholas Crawford?" James nods. "Yes, of course. He's a good friend of mine. We go surfing a lot."

"So, he wasn't at the party this evening?" I ask.

"Nope." James shakes his head. "I heard that he got stuck on the other side of the island and couldn't make it. It probably has something to do with that resort."

"What resort?" Sydney asks.

"He's one of the investors in a large resort over there and they've had a lot issues getting permits and stuff like that. It has been kind of a headache."

I nod, taking it all in. From what James says he seems like a normal guy.

Maybe I don't have anything to worry about after all.

So, why does my heart still keep skipping beats?

13

WHEN SHE INTERRUPTS ME...

After Sydney leaves, I take off my clothes, wash my face, brush my hair, and climb into bed. The long flight and the two hour drive along with the excitement and built-up anticipation of the party have all taken a toll on me. I'm not sure what time it is in Boston right now or how little I slept in the last twenty-four hours and I'm too tired to figure it all out. I turn off the lights and close my eyes.

That's when the thoughts start running through my mind. I run over every person I have known in my life, trying to remember if there's anyone by the name of Nicholas Crawford.

Nick? Do I even know any Nicks?

No, I can't say that I do. I mean, there were probably Nicks who I went to high school with, it is somewhat of a common name, but I wasn't friends with any of them.

Realizing that the fatigue of the day has somehow made my mind wired, I reach for my iPad and open a reading app. I love the feeling of a real book in my hands, but I hate having the light on and physically holding the book and turning the pages, especially when I am tired.

EBooks make everything so much easier. I can store thousands of them in my device's library and read whichever one I'm in the mood for that night.

Of course, like many women, I can't really resist the ones that are a little bit explicit. Most movies and TV shows fade to black as soon as the characters start to kiss, but in books, their stories continue. In bed... that's the best part of it, isn't it?

After all of the drama that they endure, after all of the ups and downs of life, when they finally get together...that's bliss!

I bookmark my favorite parts of my favorite novels and re-read them again. Sometimes, I like a short and dirty scene, but other times I like it when the details go on for pages and pages. And it's not all sex, it's more than that. There's the pillow talk, their laughter, their arguments. A lot of things can happen in between the sheets.

I turn to my favorite scene in a novel set in the West. They have loved each other since they were children and they sleep together for the first time in a field right next to the rushing Colorado River. The details are so exquisite that I can't help but close my eyes and smell the dry swaying grass and feel the spray of the cool water on their bodies.

My fingers slowly make their way down my own body, as I feel the contours of my thighs.

The skin is soft and inviting and I run my fingers down to my belly button. It moves up and down with each breath, quickening in tempo as my breathing speeds up.

Whatever bad thoughts I typically have

about my body all seem to disappear, or fade into the distance.

Now, I relish in it. A familiar tingling sensation starts to build up within me, starting at the tip of my toes. I flex my feet and the sensation runs up my thighs.

I'm dressed in a blush pink, soft pajama set that I bought for the trip.

Both the t-shirt and the shorts are incredibly soft and the t-shirt has delicate ruffled sleeves.

I pull the bottoms off, along with my underwear, and toss them onto the bed next to me. I prop up the iPad so that I can keep reading the words on the screen while having the use of both of my hands.

My fingers run up my shirt and touch the outline of my breasts.

I feel my nipples get hard and I arch my back from pleasure. Keeping one hand there, my other travels back down my body and my legs open wide.

They tease me by first running up the inside of my thighs, before touching the warm, wet center of my body.

I tilt my head back as my fingers start to

move in familiar circles and plunge deep inside. When I get closer and closer, my fingers speed up and my hips start to move up and down.

A knock on the door startles me. It breaks through my concentration, immediately taking me out of the moment.

For a moment, I keep my fingers where they are and just listen. Maybe it's nothing. Maybe it's just a critter walking outside. But they knock again. This time it's louder.

"Olive?" Amelia asks. "Olive! I'm sorry to bother you but I have to speak with you."

"Just a second!" I yell, hoping that she won't just let herself in. "I was sleeping."

My jaw clenches with irritation as I search around in the dark for my shorts and underwear.

I search the floor next to the bed before realizing that I had buried them under the sheets next to me.

"Yes?" I say in a very dismissive manner, opening the door.

I should be nice, but she shouldn't be bothering me at this hour.

"I'm really sorry for coming here now,

but Mr. Crawford would like to see you," she says, shuffling her feet and looking down at the floor. I stare at her in disbelief. Did she really just say this to me?

"He just got back and he requested to see you," she repeats herself.

"Now? Are you serious?" I ask.

I look her up and down. She's dressed in the same thing she was wearing at the party, but she looks different. Her hair is a bit of a mess and she's no longer wearing makeup. She was clearly roused out of bed as well.

"Yes, I'm afraid so," she says.

I consider doing it for a moment, but then I get a hold of my better senses.

Yes, he did give me a big gift.

But I traveled all of the way here to meet with him and he stood me up at the party. And now, he wants to meet me at this hour?

"No, absolutely not," I say definitively without leaving any room for negotiation.

"Please, you can't say no to him."

"Why not?"

"Very few people do," she says.

"Well, I don't work for him. He invited me here and I showed up. I was at the party, he didn't come. I will see him tomorrow but for now I need to get some sleep."

I close the door as her mouth drops open and wonder if I have made a terrible mistake.

14

WHEN I MEET HIM...

My words come out strong and powerful and self-assured but inside I feel like I'm dying. The look of concern on Amelia's face scares me.

Did I make a mistake?

Was coming here some sort of mistake in general?

Even so, there is no way that I'm going to meet him in this state.

I'm not ready.

Earlier this evening, I looked pretty and presentable.

But now?

Naked face, bed hair, no planned outfit.

My mom always taught me that first impressions are everything, and even though she has probably been wrong about everything else she ever told me, I'm certain that she was right about this.

I pick up my iPad and try to focus my mind on something else. But the book that hit the spot so perfectly only a few moments ago fails to grab my attention.

I look through my library trying to find something else to read. Eventually, I turn to another one of my favorites.

It's by Charlotte Byrd, one of my favorite writers, and it's a lot darker in tone. Ellie goes to an exclusive yacht party and decides to participate in an auction where she has to spend the night with one of the eligible bachelors.

The men are young, rich, and incredibly good looking and the money is astronomical.

Why not, right? You only live once. I turn to my favorite part where she is lying on the bed with a blindfold over her eyes waiting for the man who bought her to come in.

My mind starts to clear and my breaths start to quicken. My fingers quickly make their way down my body and underneath my shorts. I don't bother taking them off this time. This isn't going to take long. My legs open up and my butt starts to move and up and down. My anticipation builds as my fingers move in neat concentric circles around my core before making their way inside. I point my toes as a warm soothing sensation amplifies and spreads throughout my body, slowly at first and then all at once.

My breath gets caught in my throat and my heart skips a few beats before pounding so loudly that I can't hear another thing. When the moment passes, I flex my feet over and over again to get the last bit of pleasure out of my body.

It takes a few minutes for my breathing to get back to normal. I summon the little strength that I have to get up and use the bathroom before falling back into the bed.

There's another knock on the door.

What now?

I'm not going to talk to him now, no matter what she says.

Doesn't she get that?

"Amelia, I already told you, I'm not going," I say, opening the door, and the motion sensor on the porch comes on.

Instead of standing further back, he leans on the door frame, propping himself up with his left arm. His head is tilted down allowing his dark straight hair to fall into his wide sparkling eyes.

"I heard that you didn't want to see me," he says confidently.

His words catch me by surprise but I don't let that phase me. "I was at the party," I say, straightening my back. "I thought you were going to be there."

"I got held up," he explains without providing an explanation of anything.

"So...do you want to see me?" he asks. His thick pale pink lips curl at the corners, revealing little indentations in the middle of his cheeks. Those dimples make my knees weak.

"I'm here, aren't I?" I manage to say as I

watch him run his fingers along his square jaw.

If this were daylight and I'd had the proper sleep, I would've apologized for not coming to see him at night. But something infuses me with extra strength and I refuse to do that.

"Yes, you are," he says slowly, tossing his hair. It's razor straight and falls perfectly from one side to another.

I meet his eyes and force myself to not look away first. He seems to find this charming and gives a little chuckle in response.

"Well, I just wanted to introduce myself. My name is Nicholas Crawford." He extends his hand. I wipe the sweat off my palm on the back of my shorts before shaking his.

"It's nice to meet you," I say. "I'm Olive Kernes."

"Well, I'll let you get some rest now," he says.

A light breeze picks up and sways his light V-neck t-shirt, pressing it hard against his torso.

My tongue hits the roof of my mouth as I count six clearly defined abdominal muscles. Even though he is wearing a pair of loose-fitting board shorts, they fit snugly around his tight apple butt, leaving little to the imagination. I watch him disappear into the darkness.

Suddenly, something occurs to me.

"Wait!" I yell after him. "Didn't we meet before?"

He walks back into the light and smiles at me.

"At the beach, earlier today?" I ask. The sun was right behind him, blinding me, and I was too focused on my injuries to get a good look at him, but now I'm certain of it.

"Yes," he admits.

"Why didn't you say anything then?" I ask.

He takes a step back and moves his jaw from side to side.

"I thought it would be better if we met at the party but then I got called off on business."

I nod. Yet another answer without much of an explanation.

"I want you to meet me tomorrow at seven, at the gazebo overlooking the cliffs," Nicholas says, his eyes meeting mine and refusing to let mine go. "I have something to discuss with you."

15

WHEN I SEE HER...

The following morning, I knock on Sydney's door right before nine and it's the latest that I can possibly wait. She yells for me to come in, but the door is locked. Begrudgingly, she gets out of bed and stomps over to let me in.

"What time is it?" she asks.

"I don't know," I lie.

She shakes her head.

Her long straight hair falls in all directions but will only require a brief run of the brush to bring it back to its usual luster. She heads straight to the kitchen counter and starts a pot of coffee.

Her robe falls off her shoulder. She's not

wearing anything underneath yet she's not too quick about pulling it shut. One of the things that I admire most about Sydney is that she doesn't have the body of a model and yet she acts and feels like she does. Her confidence is contagious. She has big breasts, a narrow waist, and a large booty and she loves every single one of her curves.

Sydney struggled with her weight and body image immensely as a teenager, going through a series of crash diets and binge eating marathons. It didn't help matters that her mother's family are all Asian with naturally thin frames and tiny bones.

Neither of our mothers made us feel anything but shitty about the bodies that we live in, blaming us for whatever extra weight we carried as some sort of deficiency in the quality of us as human beings.

Yet, somehow, about a year ago, Sydney emerged with this completely different attitude. Instead of waiting to live her life until she lost those extra fifty pounds, she just embraced who she is right now, in this moment, appreciating the body that she wakes up in every day. That's when she started sleeping naked and walking around our apartment in nothing but a silk robe in the mornings.

I am about her size, and I try to follow suit. I know that it's wrong to hate the extra fat around my hips and the fact that my thighs don't touch. I know that I shouldn't complain about the folds that my stomach makes when I sit down. Yet, it's all I can think about.

Especially here.

At least, back in Boston, I could hide behind a heavy coat and sweaters for nine months of the year.

But in Maui? The sun and the humidity and the tropical weather makes it impossible to hide the body that I have.

What happens when I have to wear a swimsuit?

"So...how was your date?" I ask. I'm eager to tell her about Nicholas but I'm equally eager to hear about James.

She takes a sip of her coffee and flashes

a mischievous smile out of the corner of her mouth.

"All I'm going to say is," she teases me. "He's great in bed."

I put my mug down onto the counter.

"No, no, no. I need details!" I demand to know, feeling my eyes lighting up. There's nothing better than hearing a juicy story of last night's escapades.

Not that this is a normal thing for Sydney, far from it.

In fact, it was me who'd had a few one-night stands over the last two years, never to return the guys' calls again.

Sydney, on the other hand, has dated the same guy all throughout college and one year into us living together.

Their parents were already making wedding plans when he got drunk one night and confessed to her that he was gay. He comes from a strict traditional family where being gay is out of the question. In fact, he said that he still wanted to marry her and was willing to come to an arrangement where both of them would keep their lovers discreet.

Sydney told him that this was 2019, not 1879, and she would not be marrying anyone who was not one hundred percent in love with and sexually attracted to her. Given that her mother was best friends with his mother since they were young girls, her mother did not understand and even refused to accept the fact that her friend's son could be, in her words, *one of those*.

"Are you going to tell me everything or what?" I ask as Sydney takes one tiny sip of her coffee at a time.

"He took me to this beautiful cove where we walked on the beach and talked about everything from school, our work, our parents, the moon, and the stars," she says, her eyes twinkling.

"The moon and the stars?" I ask.

"Astronomy is a hobby of his. James just got this big telescope that he uses to look at everything up there," she says, pointing up. "I don't know anything about it since I got that one C in Bevler's Intro to Astronomy. But the way he talked about it, it made it sound, I don't know, interesting somehow."

"Yeah, a hot guy walking with you on the beach under the moonlight would make just about anything sound interesting," I joke.

"Oh, c'mon now, that makes me sound like a total creep," James says, walking out of the bedroom and startling me. I jump a whole foot away from her, spilling my lukewarm coffee all over myself.

Sydney starts laughing.

"You weren't going to tell me he was here the whole time?" I ask.

"Eh, I was waiting for him to scare you." She smiles.

As I clean myself off, James walks over to Sydney, puts his hand around her shoulder, and pulls her cheek close to his for a kiss.

"Hey there, beautiful," he whispers into her ear quietly so that I won't hear it.

I hang out in the kitchen with them for a while, watching them swoon all over each other. You'd think it would be annoying, or gross even, but I'm really happy for her.

She spent a long time dating someone who never made her feel good enough and then more time alone thinking that she would never feel like anyone liked her again. So, watching her now with him makes me utterly happy for her, from the inside out.

I still want to tell her all about Nicholas, but for now that will have to wait.

16

WHEN WE SPEND THE DAY TOGETHER...

W hen James goes to work, Sydney and I decide to spend the day together. We look up some stuff today and ask Amelia if we can borrow a car. She offers for Thomas to drive us but we decline.

On the drive over to the nearest hiking trail, I tell her about Nicholas and what happened the night before. I gloss over the intimate details and just focus on the fact that he first asked me to come see him through Amelia and then showed up directly at my door in the middle of the night.

"I don't get it, he just showed up?" she

asks, tying her sneakers in the passenger seat. I lost the coin toss and got the dubious honor of driving down the winding Hana Highway first.

"Yeah, and with this attitude, too. Like I owe him something."

"Well, you sort of do," she points out. I roll my eyes and turn up the music. "So, what did he look like?"

"Really, really attractive. He looked a bit like Tom Cruise in Jerry McGuire actually."

"I like him better in Mission Impossible," Sydney says.

"How can you tell the difference? He hasn't aged in decades," I joke. She laughs.

"But Nicholas is taller, over six foot two, I think. With broad shoulders. Really nice abs."

"You saw his abs?"

"He was wearing this really tight t-shirt and the breeze pushed it against his torso. Once I saw it, I couldn't look away."

Out of the corner of my eye, while trying to focus on the sharp turn around a cliffside, I see Sydney lick her lips. She has never been this exuberant or lusty. I don't know if it's the tropical heat or the physical heat between her and James but she's different here. More alive somehow.

"But I didn't tell you the whole story," I continue.

"Okay..." She braces herself by holding onto the side of the car, turning her body toward mine.

"He asked me to meet him tonight at seven at the gazebo," I say the words slowly and deliberately. I wait for them to sink in before adding the last part. "He said that he has something to discuss with me."

"What the *hell* does that mean?" she squeals in an excited, high-pitched manner.

I shrug my shoulders. "I have no idea."

I park near a small turnout, near the beginning of a hiking trail. I grab my backpack, which is stuffed with a water bottle, granola bars, and other goodies as well as an external charger for my phone, a small tripod in case we want to take any stylistic photos for Instagram, and a paper map of the area that Amelia insisted that I take. Sydney puts on her own backpack and we follow the sign leading down a small path into the tropical rainforest.

The leaves are wide, thick, and incredibly green. Only a few steps into the forest and I can barely hear the traffic outside or see the road. The leaves all around us are covered in droplets of water, as if it had just rained. A few rays of sunshine stream in, creating a kaleidoscope of light.

We walk for some time, filling the space around us with voices and laughter, and then we reach the waterfall. It comes from somewhere high above our heads, dropping the water into a small pool right at our feet. It's about the size of a small pond, but it never grows any bigger and I wonder how that is physically possible.

"Here, let me take a picture of you here," Sydney says. I groan silently to myself, thinking that she won't notice.

"C'mon. This place is beautiful. You're beautiful. Don't let this moment pass you by without a picture," she says as I take a few steps toward the waterfall and position myself into the pose that I have practiced a million times in the mirror.

I square my shoulders with her and turn my torso to the side, bending the leg that's closest to the camera. I place my hand on my waist to create the angles that all the models on social media are always photographed with.

I've always hated myself in pictures, but after I watched some YouTube videos and practiced a lot in the mirror, I memorized the position that my body should be in and now the pictures all turn out pretty well. Occasionally, I stick my head out too far back instead of elongating my neck or slouch a bit too much. But this one turns out perfect.

"There!" Sydney announces, looking back at it on her phone. "See, it's perfect!"

Yeah, I say to myself, letting out my stomach that I have sucked in until it couldn't be sucked in anymore. The pose is God-awful uncomfortable, but it also makes me look incredibly slim and photogenic. It's a small price to pay.

"So, what do you think he wants to talk to you about tonight?" Sydney asks as she strips down to her bikini and poses in front of the waterfall like a model with years of experience in front of the camera: she extends her arms to the sky, pops her back, and sticks out her butt. Her smile is effortless and relaxed and the photo comes out magical.

"I have no idea," I say, letting out a sigh.

17

WHEN I MEET HIM AT THE GAZEBO...

We get back from hiking wet and sweaty and I immediately jump into the shower. I have an hour to get ready and I have no idea what that even means. What exactly am I getting ready for? What does he want to discuss with me?

Sydney sits on the couch waiting for me to finish before taking her shower. She can just as easily go to her cottage, but we have been roomies for so long that old habits die hard.

"What are you going to wear?" she yells over the rushing water. That's the million dollar question.

"I have no idea!" I yell back.

"Did you get the vibe that he's into you?" she asks when I come out with a towel wrapped around my chest. The water from my hair drips onto the floor, making a little puddle.

"Why don't you ever wrap it up in another towel?" Sydney asks, exasperated, throwing her hands up.

We've had this discussion before, more than once. The thing is that I don't like the feel of a towel piled on top of my head. It's heavy and cumbersome, and it makes me feel like I'm about to fall over. Instead, I pick up the other towel off the counter and dry the ends.

"The hair on your head is still wet," she points out. "Unless you dry all of it and wrap it up."

I shrug my shoulders. "Can we *not* discuss this now? I have enough on my mind."

She smiles and comes over, squeezing my shoulders a little.

"C'mon," she whispers into my ear. "I'm

just trying to distract you a little. I know that you're a ball of nerves."

I nod and give her a little smile. I take a moment to collect my thoughts after she undresses and gets into my shower.

What should I wear?

It's getting dark, but the weather is just as humid and warm as it was earlier this afternoon. I don't know what I'm walking into so whatever I wear, I have to be comfortable. Nothing that pinches me or digs in anywhere. At the same time, it should be flattering.

The shoes are the easiest decision. I only brought three pairs: beige wedges, flip-flops, and sneakers. I wore the wedges to the party last night, and while they are agreeable enough, they make me feel a little bit too fancy. I know that Sydney will protest, but I'm going go with the flip-flops.

I turn my attention to my clothes. I could go with the leggings again, but they left me quite sweaty at the party. No, I need something that will let some of the breeze through. Luckily, I brought a short dark blue dress with cap sleeves. It looks nice for a dinner out, but paired with the flip-flops, it has an easy going, casual feel to it.

"You look beautiful," Sydney says, coming out of the bathroom. I smile and mouth thank you. I am glad that she does not make me second-guess my outfit more than I already am.

My hair is still damp by the time it's almost seven, but I don't blow dry it. The strands around my face make loose, beachy waves that are actually quite pretty. I do take a moment to reapply my eyebrow tint, a fresh coat of eyeshadow, another swatch of the eye liner, and the mascara. I finish my look off with a peach-colored lipstick that glistens in poor light.

"Good luck," Sydney whispers. "I'll be waiting on pins and needles to hear what happens."

She takes my hand in hers and gives me a little squeeze. My stomach makes a loud rumbling sound and I cover it to try to calm my nerves.

"It's going to be fine," she adds. "Trust me."

We promised each other that we would stop making promises that we can't keep a while ago, but I'm glad that she breaks it.

I walk down the path away from my cottage with trepidation.

I see the gazebo in the distance, in front of the house. There are lights strung up around it, and I try to remember if they were there last night.

As I get closer, I see the outline of a man leaning on the railing. As I get closer, the path turns from dirt to large flat stones. My flip-flops make a loud smacking sound with each step and Nicholas hears me approach.

"I am glad you came," he says, extending his hand toward mine and helping me up the step into the gazebo.

"Thank you," I say breathlessly, mainly as a result of my nerves.

I feel his eyes moving slowly up and down my body. There's an intensity to them, the kind that is difficult to describe. It's almost as if he were looking straight through me, through my clothes, through every armor that I put up, and into my very core.

I look at him in return.

Dressed in a black slim fitted suit, his legs look long and toned. The collar of his white shirt is starched and his tie has a tiny asymmetrical design to it.

The jacket is buttoned in the front. His shoulders are broad and his hands are back in his pockets.

The man I met at the beach, the surfer, and the man who came to my door last night seemed to have vanished completely. But then he runs his fingers along his jaw just like he did last night and I see a glimpse of him.

When a strand of hair that has been slicked back breaks free and falls into his eyes, I see another.

"I wanted to thank you again for accepting my gift," he begins.

His words are confident, strong, sharp.

"Of course, I wanted to thank you for being so generous. I mean, that's a lot of money."

"Not for me," he says without a trace of

hesitation in his voice. "I wanted you to have it."

I give him a slight nod.

"Now, let us discuss what you can do to repay your debt," he says.

18

WHEN HE ASKS ME...

I take a step away from him. The floorboard creaks under my left foot. The chirping of insects gets louder along with the heartbeat pounding near my temples.

"What do you mean?" I ask.

My whole body starts to tremble so I lean back on the railing for support.

"I did you a favor and now I would like you to do something for me," he says. His eyes meet mine. Suddenly, there's a coldness in them. A darkness even, one that I have never seen before.

Of course. How could I be so stupid?

No one does anything for anyone without wanting anything in return.

He didn't just find me sitting next to a gas station and give me a buck out of his pocket. He sought me out. He did research on exactly how much I needed.

"I thought you said that the check was a gift," I remind him.

"It is." Nicholas' eyes narrow, looking into the distance over the ink-black water.

I pull my eyes away from his and look out into the abyss before us. The moon illuminates the crescents of the waves with its cool light, but only a little bit.

Suddenly, I see a fin. One followed by another. The dolphins dive in and out of the water making a high-pitched giddy sound that makes me smile.

"I've never seen dolphins before," I admit.

"You should come out here to this spot in the mornings. You'll see dolphins, whales, birds..." he says, letting his words trail off at the end.

When he turns his body toward mine, I

know that the sightseeing portion of the evening is over.

"If something is a gift then it doesn't have any strings attached," I say.

"You don't even know what I am going to ask you to do," he challenges.

His tie gets bunched up a bit, so he unbuttons the two buttons of his jacket and straightens it.

"I don't want to even hear about it if it's something illegal," I say.

"It's not."

I clench my jaw. I feel my reasons for saying no starting to disappear.

"Why did you send me this money? How did you even know that I needed it? Did you hire a private investigator to study me?"

"Which one of those questions do you want answered first?" he asks smugly. I cross my arms around my chest and wait.

"You'd be amazed what you can find out about someone with a good private investigator, but I didn't need that. All I had to do was run your credit score. They showed all of your debt. A lot of debt."

I catch myself slouching, so I straighten my back out in defiance.

"Yes, I know that I had a lot of debt. I wanted to get a good education. So what?" I ask.

"You didn't have to accept my gift," he says, leaning back on the railing.

He has me there.

Now, I wish I hadn't.

I'm about to say something else, but he puts up his arm to stop me.

"Okay, do you want to hear what I have to say or do you want to argue with me?" he asks.

I give him a brief nod.

"I paid off your debt, every last penny," he starts. "Now, I want you to do something for me."

I wait.

"I want you to spend 365 days and nights with me," he says slowly and deliberately. "Live with me. Go everywhere I go. Business trips. Dinners with clients. You will act charming and happy to be there. The people I deal with will have to like you. A lot. Some will have to want you."

I hear all of the words that he says but my mind focuses on only one of them: nights.

"What do you mean by I have to spend 365 *nights* with you?" I ask.

"Exactly that."

"I won't have sex with you," I say categorically.

"You don't have to," Nicholas says, his eyes challenging mine. "But I promise you one thing. You will be begging me to do it before our time is up."

The words send shivers through my body, the good kind.

My tongue touches the roof of my mouth and it takes actual effort to not let it lick my lips.

I hate to admit it, but one of the reasons I even came here tonight is because of how incredibly sexy I find him.

If he were a lot older or not so attractive, I'd probably find this proposal absurd and degrading.

But with him, I feel this chemical pull toward him.

"I don't understand why you need me to

do this," I say after a moment. "I mean, couldn't you hire someone to be your girlfriend instead?"

"Isn't that exactly what I'm doing?" He tosses his hair out of his eyes, flashing a crooked smile.

"But why me?"

I ask. "Why fly a total stranger across six thousand miles to ask her to do this?"

He opens his mouth just a little bit, pressing his tongue on his lower lip. That's when it occurs to me. We are not strangers at all. He has to know me.

"How do you know me?" I ask.

Now, it's his turn to look down at the floor. Now, it's his turn to hesitate.

"You have to tell me or I won't even entertain this offer," I threaten even though I don't think that I'm really in the position to *not* consider it.

Nicholas looks up at me.

His irises grow big and dark.

He straightens his broad shoulders and folds one of his hands into a fist.

I don't know how but I sense that I'm in no danger from being with him, he's just trying to keep the anger building up in him at bay.

"You owe me a debt, Olive," he says slowly. "I don't have to explain anything to you beyond stating the terms of how you can repay it."

"I know," I concede. "I just want to know why me."

A moment passes without him saying a word. Then another. The first feels like a decade while the second feels like a century.

"If I tell you, you have to promise to not tell anyone about this," Nicholas finally says. "Not Sydney, not anyone."

I think about it and then say, "I promise."

19

WHEN I REMEMBER...

There's a bench that goes around the perimeter of the gazebo and Nicholas takes a seat. He points to a place next to him and I sit down as well.

"When we used to know each other, my name was Nicky Reed," he says. "That's my biological father's last name."

I search my memory for anyone with that last name, but nothing comes to mind.

"Do you remember a girl named Ashley Price?" he asks.

Thin, scrawny, with long red hair that she used to wear in braids like Laura Ingalls from *Little House on the Prairie*. The kids in my middle school used to tease her mercilessly for her crooked teeth and her freckled face.

I stood up for her when I could, but if you take someone's side too much in middle school the powers that rule, the popular seventh grade girls, can quickly turn against you as well. I devised another plan: we would pretend that we had work to do at the library and hide out there during lunch. Technically, eating wasn't allowed in the library but we could eat our sandwiches if we were really quiet.

"Ashley moved away when we were fifteen in the middle of the year," I say. "We were really close but she never told me that she was leaving. I was shocked when I heard that from one of the teachers."

"Our mom made her go live with our distant cousins in Mississippi because she got pregnant," Nicholas says.

Something that sounds like a helicopter taking off makes my head pound. My thoughts ping-pong back and forth between two revelations. One is that my childhood friend, Ashley, is related to this man standing before me. Two, Ashley got pregnant. I'm not sure which one to start asking about first, but my mouth has a mind of its own.

"We knew everything about each other," I say. "Ashley wasn't dating anyone. I would be the first person to know if she had a boyfriend. She wasn't even into boys. She thought she liked this girl in our math class."

I remember the exact moment when Ashley told me about having a crush on Christy. Her face turned two shades paler than usual and her whole body was shaking. She cracked her knuckles over and over again and said that she had to tell me something but she was afraid of losing me as a friend. I had no idea what she could tell me but I promised to be there for her no matter what. And I was.

"You only knew what Ashley wanted you to know," Nicholas says. "Our mother's husband, our stepfather, had been molesting her for months. And then he raped her. She was terrified of telling our mom because she knew she would blame her for seducing him."

My mouth drops open. Why didn't she tell me? She could've come to live with me. I could've protected her.

As if he can read my mind, Nicholas answers, "She didn't tell anyone until... later. She found out she was pregnant and she was terrified of both our stepfather and our mother. I tried to be there for her, but I spent most of my youth on the streets trying to get myself out of that house. Plus, she kept everything in this vault around her. She never told me anything until..."

The words are difficult for him to say.

I wait for him to gather his strength to continue. But he doesn't. Instead, he just looks away into the distance.

"What happened?" I whisper under my breath.

"Mom kicked her out of the house and sent her to Mississippi to live with not very nice people. She wanted to get an abortion, but she didn't know anyone there, didn't have a car, or money. She was all alone and scared to death."

"Why didn't she reach out to me?" I ask, tears are starting to build up in the back of my eyes. I don't know what happened yet but I can sense that it was something terrible.

"If I had known any of this before...I would have helped her. She was my sister but she kept it all from me. I didn't even know about the pregnancy. Mom just said that she was going to Mississippi to visit Mom's cousins," he says. "I should've asked why. I should've demanded some answers, but I was never really home. I hung around a bad group of guys and did anything I could to survive."

I nod.

"But it's no excuse. And not a day goes by that I don't think about..."

There is something he is not saying. It's the reason why I haven't heard from Ashley in all of these years. The lump in the back of my throat gets bigger.

I slide a few inches closer to him and take his hand in mine. I don't know if I'm doing it to comfort him or to comfort myself.

"Tell me," I say, giving him a squeeze.

Nicholas looks down at the floor.

His hair falls over his eyes.

Without letting my hand go, he says, "Ashley killed herself two days after she arrived in Mississippi. She hung herself in a closet while everyone else was watching TV in the living room of that trailer."

The ground starts to shift under my feet. I focus my eyes, but they get cloudy with tears.

"What do you mean?" I whisper even though he couldn't be any clearer.

"She sent me a long email explaining everything that had happened. Everything that she never told me," Nicholas says, looking up at me. "Our stepfather coming into her room at night when she was eleven. Mom getting drunk and then waking her up in the middle of the night and punching her to make herself feel better. The rape. The pregnancy. Mom finding out and calling her a slut for sleeping with her husband. Mom calling her a murderer for not wanting to keep her baby. Mom sending her away to live with strangers. The cousin's husband making sexual jokes about her body after her being there for less than an hour. Being horrified of being forced to give birth."

"Oh my God," I say under my breath, covering my mouth with my hand.

"Her email was like a long confession of everything that she had been keeping bottled up. At the end she wrote, *I hope this explains why I'm going to do this.* And then she hung herself."

I shake my head in disbelief.

"I was partying that night," Nicholas says. "I was drunk and high like I was every night back then, trying to deal with my own shitty upbringing in the only way I knew how. So, I didn't find out what she'd done until the next day. But by then, it was too late."

20

WHEN I TRY TO FORGET...

Nicholas and I sit there for some time, each trying to process our own grief. I bury my head in my hands and try to keep my tears at bay but they just keep coming. After a few moments, I give up trying. Ashley was my best friend and one day she just stopped going to school. I called her phone, I called her house, I talked to her mom. Her mom said that she thought I knew because they'd all moved away, but that was a lie. Whenever we spent time together, we either went out to a local fast food restaurant, the library or, on occasion, to my house. I was always embarrassed to invite her to my place, but she said that there was no way we could go to hers.

After her mom told me that they had moved away, I should've gone to her house. But I didn't even know where she lived.

Still, I should've tried to look her up.

I should've done some research.

Someone must have known something.

But I didn't.

I was devastated and I missed her and I was a kid.

The thing about going through shit is that it makes you a very self-centered person. We were friends but we never really confided in each other the way we should have.

I could've been there for her, had she just opened up to me a little bit. And given what she had been through, I now know that she could've been there for me as well.

Instead, we just orbited each other.

Never really letting one another in.

"What happened after that?" I ask, my tears still wet on my cheeks.

"My mother said she got what she deserved," Nicholas says, moving his jaw around from one side to another. "She refused to pay for her body to be transported back to Massachusetts. She said that our family didn't believe in suicide."

His words ring in my ears.

Didn't believe in suicide?

What is there to believe in? It happens. People do it all the time.

Is it an option for some people? Unfortunately, yes.

Could it have been prevented had Ashley had a different mother? A different stepfather? A better best friend. Most definitely.

"How do you know me?" I ask Nicholas.

"We met once, in passing. I gave you two a ride back from school," he says.

That doesn't seem like enough of a reason to do any of this. I wait for more.

"She wrote about you in my email," he says. "She told me not to blame myself for anything that she did. She said that there was nothing I could do to help her, but if I still wanted to help someone, I should help you."

My heart begins to pound and then to swell.

"After that I got clean. I got on my feet and I've been checking up on you over the last couple of years," Nicholas says. "You are actually doing really well."

"Thank you," I mumble, through the tears running down my cheeks.

My friend's dying wish was for her brother to help me. The clarity that she must've had at that moment is difficult for me to imagine, even now.

I'm no longer a teenager and I don't have anywhere near that kind of understanding.

Yet, she still decided to end her life. Why? Didn't she know that things would get better?

Teenagers don't have the experience of years to know that it's possible to go through a lot and still live a happy life. Life is long. Full of many ups and downs. Things get worse and then they get better.

"I didn't know how I could help you, but then I saw the loans that you had. I was in the position to help and I'd made a promise to my dead sister. So I did."

"But now you say that I owe you a debt," I say, challenging his interpretation of his charity.

The expression on his face changes. The pain that existed only a few seconds ago gets buried somewhere deep inside.

A coldness appears.

His gaze turns to ice.

"I was in the position to help you and now you are in the position to help me," he says.

"Three hundred and sixty-five days is a long time," I say. "I have a job."

"You will be compensated handsomely."

I wait for him to say a number, but he doesn't. I feel myself drawn to him. Yes, my heart beats a little faster in his company. Yes, my palms get a little sweatier. But it's more than on just a physical level. There's something more to this. My thoughts return to Ashley.

"Why do you need me to come with you

on your trips?" I ask, realizing that I don't even really know what he does for a living.

"That's my business," he says.

"Where will we go?"

"Not sure yet, but you will need your passport."

I've never been abroad, but I've always dreamed of traveling.

Am I actually entertaining this offer?

Why?

Ashley.

She brought us together. She forged this connection between us. It's not just Nicholas that I owe this debt to. I owe it to her, too. I should've been there for her and I wasn't. Perhaps, now I can do this to make some sort of amends.

Nicholas gets up and looks at the moon above.

This is a crazy thing to do: spend a year with a man I hardly know.

And for what?

What would be the point?

I stand up and lean on the railing next to him.

Our shoulders are so close they are

almost touching. I look at the way the collar of his shirt makes an almost perfectly parallel line to his razor sharp jaw.

"What do you mean that I will be handsomely compensated?" I ask.

"Did you think that the almost one hundred and sixty-eight thousand was a generous amount?" Nicholas asks.

"Of course."

"Do you have any reason to believe that I would not be equally generous if you were to do this for me?" he asks.

I shrug.

This conversation is going in loops and is giving me a headache.

"I don't know what you mean," I say. "I didn't even know that there was any money in this deal."

"There is," he says cryptically.

"Look." I turn to face him. "I can't just give up my life for a year if I don't know what I'm getting into. I can't just give up my job, my apartment, my whole existence.... for what exactly?"

"You owe me this," Nicholas says without any affection in his voice.

"You gave me a gift," I remind him.

"Then you owe Ashley."

Anger rises up deep within me. It bursts up to the surface and I taste bile on the back of my throat.

"Fuck you!" I yell at him.

A droplet of spit leaves my mouth and lands on his cheek.

I don't wait for a response.

I turn around and walk away.

There is nothing for me to consider.

There is no way I'm going to do anything he asks. Or demands.

Who the hell does he think he is?

He made a promise to Ashley to help me and he did.

I accepted his help.

From the looks of this place, the money he sent me did not put him into the poorhouse. I doubt that it even made a dent in his bank account.

"I will pay you a million dollars," Nicholas says.

21

WHEN WE LEAVE...

W hen I get to my cottage, I immediately start to pack my bag. I should not have ever come here. I need to get off this property as quickly as possible. I pick up my phone to call a ride share, or a cab, but the reception is terrible and I can barely get online.

My heart beats loudly, drowning out the thoughts spinning in my head. Nicholas wants to pay me a million dollars to spend a year with him.

A million dollars.

Is he insane, or am I?

Who the hell would pay someone that much and for what exactly? And how the hell is that a way for him to repay his debt to his dead sister?

Ashley.

The last time I saw her, she was spinning around with her arms up to the sky as rain fell on top of her. We were both laughing, the kind of infectious laugh that is both contagious and consuming. I don't remember what was so funny, but I do remember the peculiar way that the asphalt smelled as late afternoon steam rose off it.

How could that girl kill herself? She was so happy.

I shouldn't have ever taken a week off from work. I should have never unpacked my bags or hung my clothes in the closet. I should have never planned to stay here for such a long time.

What was I thinking?

It's obvious, of course. I've never been to Maui. This was the opportunity of a lifetime to see the world outside of eastern Massachusetts.

As I toss Sydney's dress into my suitcase, folding it in the middle and then rolling it into a baguette, another *shouldn't have* thought crystalizes.

I *shouldn't* have ever taken his money.

I owed a debt to the government, or rather three private companies that were servicing my debt on the government's behalf. I would pay thousands in interest over the lifetime of the loans, and if I couldn't make the payments, I would go into default.

My credit score would drop. I would have to pay a much higher interest rate for a car, were I to ever want to buy another one again. I would probably never be able to get a mortgage and buy a house.

People who spent a hundred thousand or more at casinos and financed their addictions by putting it all on their credit cards could declare bankruptcy. It would ruin their credit for only seven years, after that everything went back to normal. All debt was forgiven and it was like nothing ever happened.

But when it came to student loans, the government took another position. Congress made sure that no such opportunity existed. They wrote it into the law. You go bankrupt with any type of debt except student loans.

Still, I should not have taken his money.

It's a gift but not really. I have no idea what kind of business Nicholas is involved in, but I've seen enough movies. On this trip he asked me to spend the year with him. *But is it really a request?*

When I said no, he offered to pay me a million dollars.

Again, I said no.

What about next time?

When is he going to stop asking?

My heart jumps into my throat. No, I'm not going to wait around and find out.

I throw my bag across my body, grab my suitcase, and walk over to Sydney's cottage.

"I was waiting for you…" She opens the door, the excited expression on her face vanishing.

"We have to go," I say.

"What happened?" Sydney asks, shaking her head.

"Pack your things, we have to get out of here."

"Tell me what happened," she insists, sitting down on her bed.

I walk past her to the bathroom and start throwing all of her makeup and beauty products into the large bag sitting on the counter.

"What are you doing?" She runs up to stop me.

"We can't stay here. Pack your shit and I'll tell you on the way."

Finally, something seems to get through.

Without another word of protest, she packs all of her things. The reception is better in her cottage and our ride share arrives right when she finishes.

The mobile app says that it's going to cost $149 to get us to the airport, but I'm just thankful that there's even a driver available in the proximity to drive us all the way back there.

When we climb into the car, Sydney asks if I had checked the flights. "Are there even any flights going out tonight?"

I bite the inside of my cheek.

No, I did not.

I look down at my phone: no service. I probably won't have any cell reception for another hour if not more.

"We'll figure something out," I say. "We can even stay at a hotel by the airport if necessary."

Sydney exhales slowly.

"Are you going to tell me what happened?"

I pick at the plastic cover on my cell phone. My nails feel soft and limp from the tropical humidity. I find a weak spot on one and peel off the dry polish.

I've bitten my nails since I was a kid and only recently figured out a way to cope with that. I pull out Nail Growth Miracle, the thick clear nail polish that makes my nails thick. I quickly apply a few coats to the nail on the ring finger that I just scratched off. Something about its thick texture curbs my need to bite and pick during stressful situations, at least temporarily.

"Olive? What the hell did he do?" Sydney whispers. "Did he hurt you?"

I shake my head.

"Should we go to the police?"

"No," I say.

"So, what the hell are we doing?"

I glance in the direction of the driver. "I can't tell you *now*. I'll explain everything when we get there."

But Sydney is not satisfied with waiting. She points to her phone and mouths, text me.

I focus on the keys, trying to figure out where to start. The texts won't go through but that's probably a good thing. She'll just read them and then I'll delete them.

He asked me to stay here with him for a year. 365 days and nights.

I turn the phone toward her for her to read.

22

WHEN SHE REFUSES...

She stares at the words for a long time, reading them over and over again.

Sex? Sydney types.

No. I shake my head, trying to remember exactly how he had phrased it.

He said I wouldn't have to do anything I wouldn't want to, but he promised me that I will be begging him to do it before our time is up.

Sydney's mouth drops open.

"What the fuck?" she asks.

Why does he want you to do this? She types.

He said I owe him a debt. For him paying off my loans.

But that was a gift. Sydney types.

I shrug. I debate whether I should tell her about Ashley, but that seems like an impossible thing to get into over text.

What about your job?

He offered me $1 million to do this.

"What?" Sydney gasps.

I nod.

Why?

"I don't know," I say. It's not exactly a lie.

I don't know why he wants me to do this. He already paid his debt to Ashley by helping me. What exactly is this going to accomplish?

What does he want you to do? Sydney types.

Accompany him on his business trips. Maybe flirt with potential clients. He said I will need a passport.

Like an escort?

I guess, but no sex, I remind her.

Maybe he's really into you?

I shrug and type, *We just met.*

This doesn't make sense.

I know.

"So, why are we leaving?" Sydney asks after a moment.

Did he do something to scare you? She adds in a text.

I shrug and type, *Yeah, kind of. I refused his offer. He then offered me money. I got the feeling that it wasn't really an offer I should refuse. I didn't know what was going to happen next. I needed to leave.*

She nods.

You don't agree? I ask.

Doesn't seem like a bad offer to me, she types, adding a smiling emoji.

I roll my eyes. She wasn't there. She doesn't know how it felt. Besides, she doesn't know the whole story.

FINALLY, we arrive at the airport. I pay the driver the fare and the tip through the app and he puts our bags on the curb.

We don't have tickets and I wasn't sure which terminal to instruct him to go to, so I asked him to drop us off at the same airline which we used to fly here. There isn't a soul outside, and there is only one ticket agent at the far left corner.

As we walk over, Sydney buries her face in her phone.

"There are no more flights tonight," she says. "I really wish I had checked before you dragged me to the no service zone."

"I'm sorry but I really needed to get out of there," I say. "Let me just ask the ticket agent."

Sydney grabs my arm. Her irises are dilated and her eyes look cold.

"I followed you here because I thought that something bad had happened. I thought you were hurt."

"I was scared."

"So, he made you this offer. So what? You can say no."

"I didn't want to stay there tonight."

"Did you think that something would happen?" She challenges me.

I want to lie to put her mind at ease but I can't bring myself to do it.

"No, but the conversation we had...it wasn't...normal."

"Tell me everything," she says.

Still holding on to the handle of my suitcase with my crossover bag resting on my thighs, I tell her everything.

I tell her how he knows me.

I tell her about Ashley.

I tell her about her suicide and his promise to her.

Her death is still raw inside of me and I glance up at the unforgiving bright lights above to keep my tears at bay.

Sydney puts her bag down and places her purse on top of it. I know what she's about to ask me so I jump ahead.

"At some point, I got this feeling in the back of my neck that made my hair stand up. You know? There isn't any logical reason for it but it's your body telling you that something is wrong. That you're in danger. That's when I decided to leave."

"Just like that?" Sydney asks.

I narrow my eyes and focus in on hers. Her face is expressionless and impossible to read.

"I didn't want to be one of those women who is found lying in a ditch somewhere because she didn't listen to her intuition," I say, walking away from her.

A lump in the back of my throat grows bigger and bigger and I begin to sob. I'm angry and disappointed that she doesn't believe me, but I know myself well enough to realize that the tears are also a result of exhaustion. I haven't slept well the whole time we were here and anytime I am not well-rested I am more susceptible to emotional waterfalls.

"Olive, I'm sorry." Sydney catches up to me before I can get to the ticket agent. "I didn't mean to make you feel bad. I'm just...disappointed."

I nod.

I know how much she has been enjoying this trip and James, in particular.

She must be torn between wanting to be my friend, and to listen to my crazy intuition, and staying here a little bit longer for her.

"Are you crying?" she asks, putting her arm around me.

"It's nothing. I'm just really tired and exhausted."

"Yeah, you need some sleep," she says.

"I'll get some sleep on the plane," I say. "We both will."

She doesn't say anything in response. I look up at her. When our eyes meet, I know.

I shake my head. No, no, no. There must be something I can do to make her come.

"Please," I whisper.

Sydney tosses her hair out of her face.

"What are you going to do?" I ask.

"I'm going to get a hotel room and stay here until my return flight later this week," she says. "I'd like to see more of Maui and...James."

I nod.

"Stay with me," she pleads. "We can get an Airbnb together. He won't even have to know."

WEEKS LATER...

23

WHEN I WAIT...

I watch him start to undress me. The ground moves my feet, but it's my knees that are shaking. The temperature in the room goes up a few degrees. My breathing quickens.

I watch his fingers pick at my tank top. Nicholas slides one hand underneath. He runs his fingers over my torso, presses them against my stomach. They move up and down with each one of my breaths.

"Tell me to stop," he says.

My eyes look up to his. There's a fleck of gold in his irises that I never noticed before.

I don't want him to stop. I've waited too

long for this. My mouth doesn't cooperate. The words don't form.

A strand of hair falls into my eyes. I try to blow it away, but it comes back again and again. Nicholas reaches over and tucks it in with the rest of my hair between my head and pillow.

He runs his fingers up my left arm, tickling me slightly. He checks on the silk tie holding my wrist in place. It's still tight.

"Tell me to stop," Nicholas said earlier when he led me here.

"Tell me to stop," he said when he fastened my arms to the headboard.

"Tell me to stop," he says now when he lifts up my shirt. He waits for my answer. Again, I say nothing and let him pull it up to my collarbone.

He unties my left wrist and slides the shirt over my head and onto the other side.

Now, I lay topless before him. My breathing speeds up. My heart pounds so loudly inside my head I feel like I'm going to go deaf.

Nicholas presses his lips onto my skin and slowly makes his way toward my nipples. When he takes one into his mouth, my skin gets covered in goosebumps. A fire starts to build in the core of my body. My legs open on their own.

"Not yet," he says, pushing them closed again.

But my hips don't listen. They move up and down to their own rhythm.

"Tell me to stop," Nicholas whispers, taking my nipple in between his teeth, and biting on it ever so lightly.

I flex my toes to keep the explosion at bay. I've waited so long for this. I can't let it consume me before he's inside of me.

"You are so beautiful," he whispers, looking at my body.

Whatever insecurities I felt about it a few moments ago disappear and I suddenly see myself through his eyes.

My curves are round and voluptuous.

My stomach is soft, but strong. My breasts are round and voluminous.

I watch him admire my body and I can't help but admire his. But he's not naked yet. I want to run my fingers down his hard abs, but he's still wearing a t-shirt and my hands are tied.

I reach my head out to kiss him. He flinches away for a moment, and then presses his lips onto mine. They are soft and powerful. He takes my mouth with his. His tongue quickly finds mine and the tingling sensation in between my legs makes my back arch.

"Take off your clothes," I say through his kiss. "I want to see you."

He smiles, pulling away from me. The trance that existed only a few moments before is broken, along with the kiss.

Nicholas furrows his brow and gives me one shake of his head. No.

Sitting up on the bed, he touches the top button of my jeans.

"Tell me to stop," he says.

"No, no, no," I whisper, tilting my head back.

After unzipping my jeans, he pulls them off in one swift motion. I want my panties to come off, too. I open my legs to help him along but instead of pulling them off, he nestles his body in between and pulls my underwear to one side.

I stop breathing and wait. For his tongue. For his fingers. For his dick. For anything to touch me.

"Tell me to stop," he says.

"No," I exhale.

Nicholas runs his fingers over my thighs, toying with me. Teasing me. He's getting off on this.

Before I agreed to spend a year with him, I thought I would spend the year pushing him away.

I thought he would make his moves and I would stay strong. I never knew that I would want him this much. I never knew that he would be stronger than I am.

My hips move up and down with each invisible concentric circle that he draws on the inside of my thighs. My body is begging for him. Pleading. Now, my mouth has to do the same.

"C'mon," I say.

"What?" Nicholas smiles. "What did you say?"

I kiss him again. He squeezes my nipple

and I open my legs. He presses his lips onto the outside of my breast. I flex my toes and hold my breath.

"I need you inside of me," I whisper.

"You have to beg me," he whispers back. "Remember?"

I lift my head off the pillow and look at him.

"I made you a promise. I intend on keeping it," he says, smiling out of the corner of his lips.

"What do you mean?"

"Unless you plead, and I mean, really beg, it's not going to happen."

"I don't believe you," I say, challenging him. He shrugs, continuing to run his fingers up my thighs just close enough before pulling away.

He wants me as much as I want him. There's no way he could say no to me. I lean over to him and start to kiss him again. But he pulls away.

"I'm sorry," he says. "It's not going to happen tonight."

My mouth drops open.

"Are you going to beg?" he asks. His

eyes twinkle as he speaks, making me even more aroused.

"No," I say firmly.

"I'm sorry to hear that," he says, reaching over to the headboard and untying my wrists.

TODAY...

24

WHEN I SEE HER AGAIN...

The only ticket that I can afford, and that's using the word liberally, is five hours later in coach with two stops. My seat is narrow and cramped and everything including a glass of water comes at an additional charge. Since the ticket is so last minute, it costs close to $1300. I put it on my credit card, knowing that I will have to pay this horrible flight off for the next year.

Despite the tiny seat, the three dollar bottle of water, the passengers next to me who take up both of my arm rests, I fall into a peaceful and deep sleep. I only wake up when the wheels touch the ground in Los Angeles. I get to my next flight in a daze, take another brief nap during my two hour layover and then fall into another trance on the next flight to Chicago.

My layover there is five hours and I spend the time reading standing in the airport bookstore before grabbing a croissant and a tall black coffee from Starbucks. It is only on my final leg over to Logan International that I begin to feel somewhat normal again. Everything that happened in Hawaii seems like a bad dream. Maybe it all happened to someone else. Perhaps, it's even something that happened in a Netflix binge.

When I drop my bags on the floor of my apartment, Sydney's not here. I realize that Maui was not a dream. I head straight to my bedroom, take off my jacket and boots, and climb into bed. I sleep for the next twelve hours and when I wake up Sydney is still not here.

I TOOK a week off work for this trip and there are still a number of days left. I stay in bed until I can't stay here anymore and then I force myself to go outside. Walking along Boston Commons, I watch a duck making a zigzag pattern across the water. She darts back and forth before floating up to the edge where a little girl throws crumbs into the water.

Maybe I've been too hasty.

Maybe I shouldn't have made my decision on so little sleep.

Maybe I should've just got a hotel room by the airport with Sydney and enjoyed the rest of my vacation.

When will I ever be in Maui again? Probably never.

The girl makes a sudden move and the duck quickly swims away. No matter how much she wants the bread, she can't risk getting hurt.

Just like the girl, Nicholas didn't make any threats.

But when he said he would pay me the million dollars, I had to leave. It felt too dangerous to stay and my intuition is all I had.

Don't second-guess yourself, I say

silently. You wouldn't have enjoyed the trip if you would've stayed the rest of the week. You would've been looking over your shoulder the whole time. That's no way to take a vacation.

My phone vibrates.

I look at the screen hoping that it's a text from Sydney telling me what a big mistake I made leaving. Maybe it's even a selfie of the happy couple smiling on top of a volcano. But I'm wrong.

I'm in trouble.

It's my mother. She has been blowing up my phone ever since I left. I wrote her back once saying that I am no longer coming back to see her, and I've resisted the urge to reply each time she texts.

I NEED YOUR HELP.

HER OTHER MESSAGES were pleas and exaggerations. Most filled up almost the entire screen. All told me how much she missed me while at the same time telling me how terrible of a daughter I am. But these two catch my attention.

This doesn't sound like her. Of course, she could be using another angle to get to me. I could be falling for it all over again.

I put the phone down on the bench next to me.

I try to ignore it.

She's not my problem anymore. She's mean and full of hatred. She just wants to control me. She has money coming in from her social security and it's enough to live on. She can get around by herself and if I'm not there to abuse, then she'll just have to be nicer to the nurses that will come by (also paid by the government) and not drive them out by screaming profanities.

I pick up the phone again and click on the News app. I scroll through the headlines mindlessly as if reading the news has ever made anyone feel any better about anything.

I need to talk to you. I owe a lot of money.

My mother's texts come in as a notification on top of the screen. I read it before I can stop myself.

Despite my better judgement, I grab the keys and drive to her house. I arrive there without texting her back. She lives in a peeling row house in Charlestown, the oldest area of Boston. The Irish Mob used to run this place in the sixties and seventies but now parts of it are a desirable neighborhood with many hip city moms pushing their strollers around to yoga studios and coffee shops.

Charlestown is a lot less gentrified than other parts of the city, still making it relatively affordable. Of course, it still has dilapidated apartment buildings where the landlords don't keep up with repairs because the renters have no better options. Mom lives in one of these buildings. My brothers and I grew up in countless of these apartments, all in Charlestown and all shitty in their own ways.

Different layouts, same scenery.

Different streets. Same heating and plumbing problems.

Different neighbors. Same school district with metal detectors in the front.

When I walk into her narrow living

room, I look around at the piles of cardboard boxes and trash that she's generated since the last time I was here. The place stinks of old pizza and rotting food. I fight the urge to clean. That's *not* what I'm here for.

"Ma, it's me!" I yell.

Ever since high school, I have fought hard to get rid of my nasal Boston drawl, but being here in her presence, her name comes out as a mush without any final sounds.

I brace myself for a slew of hurtful remarks and name calling but instead her whole face lights up when she sees me.

"Thank you for coming," she says, putting down the glass she had been using to water the plants on the windowsill.

25

WHEN I FIND OUT...

I've never seen my mom like this before. I have seen her passed out on the floor covered in her own vomit after a night of drinking and partying. I have seen her writhing around in pain after her doctor cut off her opioid prescription and before I could get her a few pills from a dealer at the corner. I have seen her consumed with tears and pain, wailing and banging on Patrick's casket before it went into the ground.

The look she has today is one of total detachment. Her eyes are glassy and stare somewhere into the distance behind me. While they are usually quick to meet mine and make me cower, this time they barely make eye contact.

"What's going on?" I put my arm around her. "Ma?"

"I thought that this time I would win for sure," she finally says. "I was certain of it."

"What? What do you mean?"

She picks up the cup of coffee off the windowsill and picks at the W in *World's Best Mom*. Patrick made her this cup when he was in elementary school and it's her most precious possession.

"What are you talking about, Mom?" I ask.

She nods toward the iPad. I turn it on. I already know what she did, just not the extent of it.

Her favorite online poker room turns on. A pop-up urges me to put up more credit to play another hand.

"How much money did you lose?" I ask, holding my breath. I have to inhale before she answers.

"Thirty-thousand," she says slowly, chewing the words in her mouth as if they were one of her cigarette butts.

"Thirty-thousand dollars?" I gasp. "Oh, Ma. No."

"Yesterday," she says quietly.

I don't know if I heard her correctly.

"What are you talking about?"

"I heard from this forum that this one game was a sure thing. It was supposed to be rigged. It was a secret forum and only a few people knew about it. We all play together. We all share the profits."

I stare at her in disbelief.

I knew that my mom enjoyed gambling, going down to Atlantic City.

I knew she dreamed of going to Vegas someday, but I always thought that she just played the slots. Poker?

"We were going to make eighty each. But only if we all put in thirty. I didn't have the money," she says, looking out of the window. "My credit cards are all maxed out."

"What did you do?" I ask.

She shrugs. Rummaging through the pocket of her bathrobe, she pulls out a lighter and throws a cigarette in her mouth.

I wait for her to take a long drag.

"I had to ask Marlo for the money," she says, exhaling slowly.

She uses the word had as if there was no other choice. As if the sentence is as natural as *I need oxygen to breathe*.

A lump forms in the pit of my stomach.

"You didn't have to," I say.

"I did. This was a sure thing. We were all going to make money and I would be able to pay off all of my debts, including my medical bills."

The only problem is that whenever someone says something is a sure thing, it's not.

"What happened?"

"It worked. At first. But then the poker website found out about it," she says. Imagine that. "They closed our accounts. They didn't explain anything, they just sent me this form letter saying that my account is closed as a result of an irregularity."

That's one way to put it.

"Someone must've tipped them off. Maybe someone who lost money."

I look down at her hands. They are

balled up in fists, with the whites of her knuckles showing.

"This shouldn't have happened," she insists. "We've done it before and it worked."

My mouth drops open.

"What do you mean?" I ask.

"We did it a week earlier. We each put in seven thousand. We each won twenty."

I don't know how the details of this particular scam work but I have a feeling it goes something like a normal pool hall hustle. A hustler comes in, loses a round, makes everyone around the table feel comfortable with the fact that they suck, and asks for another chance to win their money back. A false sense of security makes it impossible for the others to resist taking the sucker's money again. Only this time, the hustler wins. Big.

"Why Marlo?" I ask.

"I can't get any more credit. I haven't paid my minimal payments in months. You should see all of my past due bills," she says, defensively.

"Why didn't you make your payments?" I ask.

"I don't have any fucking money, Olivia!" Mom snaps.

I knew that she had medical bills but I didn't realize that her credit cards were maxed out. I didn't know things were this bad.

"You could've told me," I say quietly.

"I know everything that you have done for me. You've done enough," she says, shaking her head.

It's words like this that make me forgive her for every goddamn awful shitty thing that she has ever done or said to me. She buries her head in her hands. I wrap my arms around her.

"Why Marlo?" I repeat my question.

"Who else is there?" Mom shrugs, her shoulders slope down as she slides onto a rocking chair.

She's right. Around these parts, there is no one else.

Marlo is the Alpha and the Omega.

The First and the Last.

She's the Beginning and the End.

There used to a number of different bookies and organized crime bosses but as Marlo consolidated power, the others were either swept under her wing or taken out completely.

"So you borrowed thirty-thousand from her?" I confirm.

"I borrowed more."

I take a deep breath and ask the question that has been sitting on the tip of my tongue the whole time I've been here.

"How much do you owe her?"

Mom looks down at the floor. Her stringy hair covers her face.

"Mom?" I prod.

"Fifty-thousand dollars," she says quietly.

26

WHEN I TRY TO FIGURE OUT
SOMETHING...

I've never seen Marlo before, but I've lived in this neighborhood long enough to know which rumors to believe and which to ignore.

She is charming and effervescent and likable and cruel and unforgiving. She has a long memory and likes to hold a grudge. The people who pay their debts, get a smile and a pat on the back, and an offer of another debt. The others?

Some are lucky to get away with a broken ankle or knee. After, they still pay the principle and the interest. Others, who can't pay at all, are never heard from again.

Mom never told me this, but Owen did.

It was the night before he went to prison. He hung out with me that night, which was unusual, and drank too much, which wasn't. We sat and talked for a long time. After a while, he told me the truth about Dad.

I always thought that he just walked out on us one day. Got sick of fighting with Mom. Got sick of her yelling at him for spending his whole paycheck at the bar. But, according to Owen, Dad owed Marlo fifteen thousand dollars. He liked to bet on the ponies and, just like Mom, he heard that one was going to be a sure thing. The race would be fixed that day and this one horse was going to win.

Well, something happened, either he had the wrong intel or they lied to get him to bet big. He lost all of the money that he'd borrowed from Marlo. He couldn't pay her one week. He couldn't pay her another. On the third week, he went out for a carton of milk and never came back.

We called the police.

We filed a missing person's report.

His picture was on the 10 o'clock news that night.

But nothing came of any of that.

Mom told me that he just left and I believed her. Then Owen told me that Marlo had him killed. Either way he never came back again.

"Why do you owe her fifty instead of thirty?" I ask, trying to get the full grasp of what has happened.

"I already borrowed another twenty-thousand two days prior and lost it. I had no way to pay that off without going in on this," Mom says. "I thought I would be able to pay off the whole fifty when I won and still have thirty left over for my own bills."

"When do you have to pay?" I ask.

"Thursday."

"In two days?" I gasp.

She nods.

"I don't know what to do, Mom. I don't have this kind of money."

"I know you don't, but what about credit? You must have some credit."

I'd run over the credit card limits of my five cards. Two are maxed out and the other three only have a limit of three thousand each.

"I don't have anywhere near that amount."

"I don't know what to do, darling," she says.

I can't remember the last she called me that.

"Maybe you can...disappear? Go somewhere and lay low for a while. Until, this whole thing blows over," I say, thinking out loud.

"Where can I go? I don't have any money."

"It will take a lot less money for you to start your life somewhere else under another identity than to pay Marlo back," I say, with an idea starting to brew in my head.

"You always wanted to go out west. Texas. New Mexico. Arizona. Wherever. You can stay in cheap motels on your way out and then get a weekly rate somewhere far away. I can get some money together for a studio apartment for you. I can rent it under another name."

Yes, this is possible.

This isn't the end of the world. Or the end of her life.

Maybe that's what Dad should've done. Marlo has a big name and a lot of power around Boston, but that doesn't mean that she has enough connections or people to find someone hiding out in a dusty one-horse desert town near Tucson.

"It will take me a week or so but I can send you a fake driver's license, maybe even a passport. I will send you some money," I add.

Mom considers this. I take it as a good sign that she's even thinking about it because she has never been further away than New Jersey. She knows how to drive but hasn't had a car in years. And now she's actually contemplating driving alone across the country.

"What about my prescriptions? I have to go to my doctors every month to get them filled."

If there's something she can buy at those truck stops along the way it's opioids, but Mom has never made a drug deal in her life. She always left that kind of dirty work to her kids. Her diabetes medication gives me pause. That's going to be harder to find.

"I'll get you new identification," I say. "I know a guy who does really good work. You'll just have to tell them that you don't have insurance and pay for them out of pocket."

"What if the doctor discovers that I have a fake ID? What if the pharmacy does? Then they'll call the cops and the whole thing will be up."

Well, not exactly because the cops aren't exactly Marlo, but it's not going to make things easier.

"It's the only way I see around it, Mom. It's the only thing you can do."

It's a lie and I hope that my face doesn't betray that. It's not the only thing I can do. I can also call Nicholas. His offer will probably still be on the table. I can make this whole thing go away with one phone call.

But I'm tired of making sacrifices so that my mother can sit on her butt and do nothing. If she's really afraid of Marlo, I need to see it.

"I will get you more pills tonight. They will tide you over for a week or two," I say. "It will take you a few days of driving to get out there. I'll get you a new phone and you can call me and tell me where you are. I'll find you an apartment. Where do you want to go? Arizona? You've always wanted to see the Grand Canyon."

"No, there must be another way," she says, shaking her head.

"If you have one, I'm all ears," I say.

Mom looks up at me with her pleading doe eyes.

"What if you just go work for her?" she says. "She asked about you again."

27

WHEN SHE PUSHES ME...

I bite my tongue, trying to keep the anger boiling up inside of me from exploding to the surface. My hands ball into fists.

"Don't look at me like that," Mom says, raising her eyebrows. "You're not that innocent."

Beads of sweat soak into the shirt underneath my arms. How does she know?

"I don't want to embarrass you, honey," Mom says sweetly. I can almost taste the saccharine in her voice. "But, c'mon, would it be such a big deal? You are a pretty woman. New girls in the neighborhood always fetch good prices. You could have this worked off in two months tops."

My index finger runs over the knuckles of my other hand, feeling the smoothness of the taut skin over the cartilage.

I don't know the extent of what my mother knows about what happened back then.

Ashley had just left and an older girl from school befriended me. I never had money for anything, not like her. She didn't have rich parents, but she had the right shoes, the right jacket, the right jewelry. The only right thing I had was a leather jacket that I tried on in the store and walked out with, without paying.

Beyond all the material things, this girl also had Tyler, the right boyfriend, at least that's what I thought at the time. He drove a red BMW convertible with the roof down, even in the middle of a Boston winter. He smacked her on her butt and said funny things to her friends.

"I don't know why I have to tell you this, Mother, but I am not going to prostitute myself so that you can pay off your gambling debt," I say sternly.

"I came to you for help, Olive. I need your help."

"And I'm here for you."

"No, no, you're not," Mom says, shaking her head. "I can't just run away. I can't drive away from here and start my life somewhere else. My life is here."

"There are people who live elsewhere. You'll make new friends. This is what you have to do when you fuck up," I say. "You can't just have Owen and me clean up your shit all of your life. At some point, you'll have to grow up."

Mom looks frail sitting in her rocking chair.

When I was a child, I didn't think she was scared of anything. I thought that she was fearless because she was so mean. But now I know that what made her so mean was that she was afraid of her own shadow.

"Leaving the state will be good for you," I say. "You'll finally get to see the real world out there."

"You're talking to me as if you've ever been anywhere yourself," Mom says.

I shrug. "I'd like to."

"So, why don't you fucking go?"

"Because I have to babysit you. I have to be here cleaning up your vomit and your literal and metaphorical shit, Mom. Without getting anything so much as a thank you in return."

"You want a *thank you,* you ungrateful little bitch?" she asks. "For what exactly? I raised you for eighteen goddamn years. I changed your diapers. I wiped your snot. I rocked you to sleep. And I never even wanted you in the first place. Your *father* made me keep you. Your *father* was the one who wanted a girl. I never wanted you. I never wanted anyone but Patrick."

Her words are like slices of razor blades against my heart.

"Yes, we know that." I roll my eyes trying to keep my tears away.

Don't break down in front of her.

Don't do it, Olive.

Mom gets off her rocking chair and

walks up to me. She stands so close to me I can hear her wheeze as she breathes.

"Listen to me," she says. "I am not going anywhere. This is my home. This is where I live. But *you*, you're going to do something for me."

I start to inhale, but she grabs me by my shirt and my body shuts down just like it used to when I was a kid.

"Your friend, Samantha, has moved up in the world. She's got a spot in Beacon Hill now, servicing senators, congressmen, and hedge fund managers. It's all discreet and you are the type of girl who is right up her alley. Educated. Without a trace of that accent that everyone tries to get away from. She gives her cut to Marlo but she pays her girls well. Real well. More than you get paid at that stupid job of yours."

After letting me go, Mom straightens my shirt with her hand.

"How do you know all of this?" I ask.

"People in this neighborhood like to talk. Especially her mom."

You'd think that nothing would surprise me now, but my mom's knowledge of Sam's business practices sends a shock wave through me.

My mouth drops open.

In high school, Sam met up with men in motel rooms and Tyler stayed out front making sure that she didn't get hurt. Even back then she had her sights on something bigger. I was the first girl she tried to recruit. She would take half of my fee in exchange for setting the whole thing up.

The one and only time I went to that seedy motel room on the outskirts of town was when we got evicted and I came home to find all of our belongings on the curb.

Mom never bothered to tell me that she hadn't paid the rent in months.

Instead, she just said to pack a bag and go stay with a friend. I called five of them, but the only one who took me in was Sam.

I was hungry, I had no money, and my college applications were due in a week.

A snowstorm was supposed to blanket all of New England with feet of snow in the coming days and the weekly rent at the motel was $250.

If I wanted a roof over my head so that I

could finish my essays and get the applications in on time, I needed to take Sam up on her offer. She promised me $300 for a night's work.

"C'mon now, Olive. You never know, maybe you'll even make a connection with one of them. You are pretty easy on the eyes when you try even if you could stand to lose forty pounds. But some men like that kind of thing."

Mom's words come in one ear and go out another. I hear her but my mind is somewhere else.

I remember how much my body shook that time I walked up to the door.

My boots made a loud clinking sound on the pavement and the bracelets Sam made me wear jingled when I knocked.

My face was smothered in so much makeup that I could practically feel it caked on my skin. My lips tasted of chemical cherry lip gloss.

"You can work the appointments around your schedule," Mom says, taking my silence as acquiescence.

The guy who opened the door was a

few years older than I was. He was a senior when I was a freshman, but I didn't know him well.

Even then I knew that Sam was just trying to break me in softly.

"Look, this isn't going to be that bad," she said. "He's not old or gross or a total stranger."

It worked for a moment and I walked inside. But then he came closer to me. All he had to do was touch my hair and I turned around and fled.

Luckily, the snowstorm caused power outages around the Northeast forcing the city to create additional shelters to provide temporary housing for everyone who lost heat. I got a cot and spent my week going to school and working on my essays, doing anything to take my mind off the path that I'd almost gone down.

I walk out of the room without saying a word.

"Where are you going?" Mom hollers after me.

"I'm not an escort. I'm not a prostitute, and I'm not a streetwalker. And if I were to ever have sex for money, I surely would never do it on your account."

She stares at me, dumbfounded. Grabbing my bag and walking out of the door, I add, "I told you what you can do to get out of this mess that you got yourself into. I told you how I would help you."

28

WHEN I SEE HIM AGAIN...

I spend the next two days trying not to think about what my mom had asked me to do for her. It would be a lie to not admit that there are moments when I waiver in my decision.

She may have asked me to prostitute myself, but she only did that because she is desperate.

Marlo is not someone you fuck around with.

She's not someone you *don't* pay your debts to.

Her request was insulting, but she only asked because she thinks I don't have any other options.

She doesn't know about Nicholas.

She doesn't know about his offer.

My thoughts return to Maui. The soft breeze coming off the ocean. The luscious peach colored flowers growing out of every bush. The way the palm trees remain constantly in motion.

If I had stayed there for just a little bit longer, then I wouldn't be dealing with this shit right now.

If I had stayed there for a little bit longer, I could've found out more about Nicholas.

Who is he, really?

Sydney stays in almost constant contact with me, putting my mind at ease for leaving her.

She sends texts, pictures, and videos doing everything that I've dreamed of doing in Hawaii: snorkeling with brightly colored fish, swimming in clear blue waters, laying out on the white sand. James is there with her in all of the pictures and, in the latest one, so is Nicholas.

Nicholas and James are tossing a frisbee around in the background of Sydney's selfie. They are on the sand and he's wearing only a pair of board shorts.

They hang low on his long defined torso, revealing the protruding muscles in the form of a V going down into his pelvic region.

My mouth waters a little bit as I zoom in on him and look at the way the light wraps around each one of his abs.

Wish you were here, Sydney texts.

What are you doing with him?

James invited him for lunch to his house. I'm making salad!

Her texts are both informative and without substance.

Why are you spending time with him?

Why is he there?

Didn't you read a word I wrote?

I call her, but the call goes to voice mail.

Instead, she sends a canned response: *Sorry, can't talk now.*

My heart skips a beat. Something's wrong.

Are you okay? I text.

Of course! Just about to sit down for lunch. Call you later.

I go over everything that happened that night.

Could I have been completely wrong about him? Yes, he did scare me a bit. His request was unusual and out of line.

But was I actually ever really frightened? Did I ever think that he would actually hurt me?

I didn't get much sleep.

There's a good chance that my intuition was driven by insomnia and its radar was off.

Or maybe this is just a ploy.

Nicholas and James are friends. He knows that Sydney is my friend.

Maybe he's just using her as a way to get closer to me.

But why? Why me? Why is he so interested in *me*?

There's a knock on the door.

It startles me. I'm not expecting anyone and I immediately think that it must be my mother. But she has never even stepped foot in here. I'm not even sure if she knows my address.

"Who is it?" I ask, looking through the

peephole. He's in his forties with short dark hair and dressed in a casual jacket and slacks.

"I'm one of the managers of the building. We've been having some issues with the boiler and I'd like to ask you a few questions."

As soon as I open the lock, he pushes the door in my face and closes it behind him.

"What the hell are you doing?" I ask.

He shoves a revolver in my face.

My eyes stare down the barrel of the gun.

Everything else becomes a blur.

"Your mother said that I'd find you here," the stranger growls.

"What do you want?" I ask, moving my head away from him.

He presses the gun to my cheek again.

A sweet smell of iron and sweat permeate through my nostrils.

"She owes Marlo a big debt."

"So what?" I ask, brazenly.

"She can't pay it."

"That's not my problem," I say.

That's partly true.

The other part is that I don't want him to know that I care about my mother at all.

In his business, feelings are leverage. He's got plenty without me giving him anymore.

"Well, neither can she, so I thought I'd make it your problem," he says.

I cross my arms and pop my hip out to give myself as much attitude as possible.

"My mother and I are not on good terms. So, I don't know what exactly your game plan is here but I don't owe anyone any debt."

He stares at me for a moment, and then exhales and lowers his gun. He reaches into his front pocket, pulling out a card.

"We are holding your mother in an undisclosed location," he says. "You have five days to come up with fifty-thousand dollars. If you don't come up with it, they'll never find her body for you to bury."

29

WHEN I ASK FOR HELP...

He hands me a card with the name Shephard Sudler and a phone number on it.

"That's my cell, call me anytime you get the money together. Your mother will only be safe for the next five days. No extensions."

"What do you expect me to do to come up with this?" I ask, shaking my head.

"You're a smart girl, figure it out."

He turns around and walks toward the door.

"How am I supposed to get it to you?" I ask.

"I accept only cash. But I will drive

anywhere in the tristate area to pick it up, if necessary," he says and closes the door behind him.

I drop Shephard's card on the table and melt into the couch.

What a clusterfuck!

I should feel angry instead I feel nothing.

I stare into the distance at some point in the corner of the room.

I can't even bring myself to feel scared for her.

She has been a disappointment all of my life and yet I keep going back and helping her. When I walked out of her apartment, I was so certain that I'd cut off ties. I was so certain that she would go on the run and maybe escape her crappy little life once and for all. Now, I know that was nothing but a dream. A fantasy.

My mother is never leaving Boston.

My mother is not one to think outside the box to solve a problem.

She's not one to take a chance.

She gambled and drank and did drugs her whole life thinking that was the only way to make her life better. But you can't keep doing the same thing over and over again and expect different results. That is the definition of insanity.

But what now?

I can do nothing and just let things take care of themselves.

Let Marlo do to her what she probably did to my father.

Perhaps that would serve her well. Perhaps that is what I should do, just cut my ties with her once and for all. But there's a child inside of me that just can't let the adult in me do that.

I can't give myself permission to let her perish. Especially since I do have another way.

Sydney.

Sydney's family on her mother's side is incredibly wealthy and generous. She has been saving up her allowance to start her business but she might lend it to me if I were to explain what's happening.

Later that evening, she returns my call. We connect over video chat and she turns the camera away from her to show me the beautiful aquamarine water, her toes buried in the white sandy beach, and the enormous margarita in her hand.

It's not lost on me that if I had stayed then it wouldn't be up to me to save my mother from Marlo's henchmen.

"I'm so jealous," I say.

"I'm having an amazing time!" Sydney squeals.

"Where are you?"

"I stayed at a hotel that first night but I've been at James's house since then. He invited me over and I never left."

Her skin is a few shades tanner making her teeth even more pearly white than usual. She's wearing her hair in two braids. She doesn't have an ounce of makeup on and she has never looked more beautiful.

"So what's going on with him? Are you two dating?"

"Yes, more than that. We're talking about moving in together."

"What?" I gasp. My mouth drops open.

"I mean, I have no idea how that's even possible but we both want to. I mean, he asked me to stay."

She doesn't say anything more, just smiles from ear to ear.

"And?" I prod her.

"I don't know. If it weren't for my job, then yes, I'd stay," she says, shrugging.

I clear my throat to remind her of another obligation.

"You, of course, you!" Sydney laughs. "But you're my best friend, nothing is ever going to change that." She sends me an air kiss.

"You moving six thousand miles away across six time zones might put a damper on our evening Netflix marathons," I say.

She nods, trying not to smile. But she can't.

I laugh.

"I'm really happy for you, Syd," I say.

I ask her to tell me more about James and she tells me about his job at the hospital and the pediatric clinic that he volunteers at in his spare time to help out the poor families on the island who can't afford medical care.

"He just really loves his job," Sydney

says. "I haven't met anyone like him before."

"What about your job?" I ask.

She might not like the particular lab or the people who work there but she believes in what she does and I can't imagine her giving it all up to live on an island in the middle of the Pacific.

On the other hand, recently, everyone (including me) has been doing things that are difficult to imagine.

I try to find a gap in the conversation in which I can bring up my particular predicament but when it doesn't come, I just blurt it out.

"Sydney, I need your help."

"What's going on?" she asks, sitting back in her chair. The rain starts to fall behind her and I hear it splatter against the roof.

I don't know where to start so I begin with the guy who shoved a gun in my face. I go into detail over my mother's debt and save the request for last.

"I have five days to get Shephard fifty-thousand dollars. Otherwise they're going to kill her."

Sydney rubs her temple and stares vacantly into the screen.

"I'm telling you this," I continue, "because I was wondering if you could lend me the money."

30

WHEN I WAIT...

Sydney looks at me. The distance that separates us no longer exists. It's just her and me, talking, sitting curled up on the couch together.

"That's a lot of money, Olive," she says as a matter of fact. There isn't a tinge of attitude in her statement.

"I know." I nod. "I wouldn't be asking if I had any other way. I tried to apply for a bigger credit limit but I can't get anything more than another two grand. I don't know what to do."

I stare into her almond shaped greenish-black eyes.

Anyone else would ask why I'm doing this.

Anyone else would say that this is your mother's problem and after everything that she has put you through you should just let her deal with it.

Well, I did.

And this is what it has come to.

I open my mouth and words just spill out.

I tell Sydney about my plan for her to drive away. Go out west. Live in a string of cheap motels under a new name.

This plan would've worked.

This plan was the one that I should have insisted on her taking.

I don't know who picked her up, whether it was Shephard Sudler or some other man who works for Marlo.

What I am certain of is that they didn't have to go far to find her. They probably found her at home or buying cigarettes at the corner store.

Since she doesn't like to drive, those are the only two places she would've been.

Since she doesn't like to drive, she didn't want to go on the run.

She didn't want to take a chance and help herself. That has been my mom's modus operandi her whole life.

She never had a steady job, relying instead on my father and complaining when he'd spend the little money that he did bring in. After he left, she did work at a few places, mainly retail and as a housekeeper, but those positions never lasted long.

The day that I started college, I took the train to Wellesley alone. Putting my suitcases on the floor of my dorm, an overwhelming sigh of relief swept over me.

Tears started to roll down my face and my new roommate's mom wrapped her manicured fingers around my shoulders and told me that homesickness was a very normal thing and that I could call her anytime I needed a mom to talk to.

She thought I was crying for the same reason everyone else was, but the truth was I was crying because I was finally away from *her*.

My mother's lack of inertia is contagious.

Why do anything when nothing is ever going to work out?

Why take a risk?

Why even do the bare minimum when you could just wait and maybe someone else will do it for you?

When I was in elementary school, she would hit me for getting a C on a test. When I got to high school, she would mock me for studying too hard.

Most of the time, someone did show up to help her out of the messes that she'd made. At first, it was my dad. Then Patrick. Then Owen. And then me.

And now?

The one time that I actually walked away from her, everything became much worse.

If I had forced her into the car, if I had even driven her out of town myself, set her up in some studio apartment somewhere in Texas, then Shephard Sudler wouldn't be handing me his card.

But because I walked away once, her death will be on my hands.

Sydney doesn't ask why I'm asking her for this money because Sydney knows the guilt that I feel. Instead she says she'll call me back after she sees how much money she has in her account.

The rain stopped, leaving beads of water on the outside of my window. One droplet begins to roll down in a zigzag, colliding with another one and building up steam. Now traveling with great mass they bulldoze their way down the glass consuming unsuspecting droplets along their path.

A few hours later, my phone rings. I take a deep breath as I press the Accept button.

"I don't have enough," Sydney says. "I only have seventeen thousand I can get on my credit cards as an advance and my mom refused to even entertain giving me a loan. I have another six that I saved up for my business but that's it."

With my three thousand that's still twenty-four short. I can perhaps use this money to buy more time, but what's that going to get me? Another few days is not going to make all of this money magically appear in my account.

"You know what you have to do," Sydney says.

I nod. I don't want to even think about it.

"I don't even know if his offer still stands." I shrug.

"You have to ask."

I move my jaw around and bite the inside of my lip.

"What's he like?" I ask. "You had lunch with him, right?"

"He's actually really great. Fun. James is really close friends with him."

I nod.

"Charming. Has lots of interesting stories to tell. Plus, he's quite easy on the eyes."

"I know that part," I say, smiling out of the corner of my lips.

"This isn't such a terrible option, Olive. I know that things didn't go well between you two back there but why not give it a chance?"

"Wait a second." Something occurs to me. "You're not just saying that because you want me to come to Hawaii with you, are you?"

Sydney's eyes light up.

"It could be fun. I mean, think about it. When was the last time we did anything reckless?" she asks. "We've both worked really hard to get into this super prestigious college and then majored in really hard subjects while everyone else seemed to just party. Then we started working right away...maybe we're due for a break. Just some time off with some hot guys in the most beautiful place in the world?"

"You make it sound so...carefree." I laugh.

"I'm just trying to put a positive spin on a pretty shitty situation," she admits.

"I know." I nod. "I appreciate it."

"Are you going to do it?" Sydney asks after a long pause.

31

WHEN I MAKE THE CALL...

Sydney gets Nicholas' number from James and I jot down the digits on a piece of scrap paper. After we hang up, I stare it for a while, running my fingers on the rugged edges, trying to decide what to do.

It feels like I have a choice, but I really don't.

He is the only one who is in the position to give me this money.

Can I do it?

Can I take him up on his offer?

Can I do it for *her*?

No matter how I would like to spin it in my own mind, no matter how much I would like to pretend, calling Nicholas would be doing it for her.

The stakes may be higher. I am not coming over and helping her with the laundry while listening to her criticize me.

I'm not just paying her share of the rent.

I am saving her life.

And as much as I want to be done with her, to kick her out of my life for good, I am not willing to let her die, especially if there's something I can do to prevent it.

I dial Nicholas' number slowly and add him to my contact list.

Then I press the big green button and wait.

"Nicholas Crawford," he says, answering on the third ring.

I can't believe he is actually one of those obnoxious people who answers a call by saying his name.

"Um...this is...Olive Kernes," I say, keenly aware of just how many pauses I took to get this sentence out.

"How are you?" he asks without missing a beat. I'm surprised by how unsurprised he seems to hear from me.

I want to hang up immediately.

I look away at the screen and contemplate pushing the red button.

Hang up.

Hang up.

It's not worth it.

"Olive?" I hear him on the other side. "Don't hang up."

"I don't know why I'm calling."

"Yes, you do."

"Do you?" I ask.

"I may have an inkling of an idea."

I put him on speaker phone and crack my knuckles.

"I enjoyed spending time with your friend Sydney."

My body tenses up.

I can't quite pinpoint it but he has some sort of effect on me.

His voice energizes every cell in my body and there's nothing I can do to calm them back down.

"She said she had fun, too," I say slowly.

"James is a really good friend of mine," Nicholas adds.

I know what he's doing.

He's trying to put me at ease.

If Sydney likes him, if her boyfriend is close friends with him, that means I can trust him. That means nothing bad can happen.

But is that enough?

"Do you know what happened to my mother?" I ask.

I didn't tell Sydney to keep this quiet, but I wouldn't be surprised if James already knew and then told Nicholas.

"No, is she okay?" he asks, his voice is marked with concern.

I inhale deeply.

"She's in a lot of trouble. She borrowed money from the wrong person and now she can't pay any of it back." I bite my lower lip and pause.

Nicholas waits for me to continue.

"They're holding her hostage until I pay her debt," I finally come right out with all of it. "They are going to kill her if I don't come up with the fifty-thousand."

"What's your bank account number?" he asks without waiting for me to ask.

"Um..."

"Look it up," he instructs.

I click on the banking app on my phone, sign in and read off the number.

A moment later, my phone beeps.

A notification appears.

He has deposited fifty-thousand dollars into my bank account.

Another notification: the money is already in the account.

Apparently, he wired it from such an account that the bank doesn't need the normal three days to process it and make sure that there's money there.

"Wait...I didn't even...I'm...thank you," I finally say. "Thank you so much."

"You're welcome."

I don't know what else to say. I wish that we were on video chat so that I could at least look at his face and thank him in person.

"Nicholas, are you still there?" I ask after a moment even though I can hear his quiet deep breaths on the other side of the phone.

"Yes," he says.

He's waiting for me to take the initiative.

But I am too taken aback by what he has just done to put together a coherent sentence.

"Thank you so much." My words come out hesitantly, but I'm thankful they come out at all.

"You're welcome," he repeats himself.

"Why...why did you do that?"

"You needed help."

"But what about...your offer?"

"That has nothing to do with this."

My shoulders slope down.

I slouch in my seat.

My mind doesn't understand what he means.

"You don't want me to spend the year with you?" I ask.

"That's not what I said," he says. His voice is even and without much affection.

"What does that mean?" I ask. "I don't understand."

"I want you to spend the year with me. But that has nothing to do with this money. Your mother's life is in danger. I can help her with a swipe of a few buttons. That's what I did."

"Thank you," I say. "You're so...generous."

"Anyone in my position would do the exact same thing."

"No." I shake my head. "No, they wouldn't. I just wish there was something I could do to repay you for your kindness."

"If you insist, there is something you could do."

I wait for him to explain.

"I'd like to have dinner with you tomorrow night. There's a beautiful restaurant in downtown Maui that I think you'd adore."

My heart skips a beat.

"Will you have dinner with me, Olive?"

32

WHEN I HAND OVER THE
MONEY...

Now that I have the money, I am not entirely sure how to make the exchange. I glance over at the five envelopes of cash that I retrieved from the bank earlier today.

I can give Shephard Sudler the money, but how does that guarantee my mother's safety?

I don't know anything about him except that I can't trust him. This is a lot of money and I need assurances that my mother will be released.

I message a few people on Facebook and then call the number that one of them gives me.

"Samantha?"

"Yes, how may I help you?" Her voice sounds peppy and upbeat as if she were a customer service representative at a five-star hotel.

She doesn't have a trace of her old New England accent and each word comes out crisp as if she were a polished, wealthy woman. I guess that's exactly what she is now.

"This is Olive Kernes, I need to speak with you."

Sam and I meet at a Starbucks in Harvard Square. We hug, tell each other how wonderful we look, and then both order lattes.

Samantha has long caramel hair, a trim yoga body, and flawless skin. Dressed in leggings, boots, a figure-hugging jacket, she looks like a regular suburban mom stopping in for an afternoon pick me up. Little does anyone around here know that she is the most connected madam in the Northeast.

At least that's what my research told me. Once my mother made her suggestion,

I couldn't resist finding out more about my old friend.

"It's nice to see you again," she says as we make small talk about our lives after high school. But when the conversation hits a lull, I don't waste any more time.

"I know that you work for, or with, Marlo," I say.

She doesn't respond, giving me neither a confirmation nor a denial. There's no point in being indirect. She won't help unless I tell her the truth.

"My mother owes her a debt, which I'm going to pay on her behalf," I start. "Someone who claims to work for Marlo wants me to pay him directly, but I don't know if he actually works for Marlo. I need to get in contact with her directly."

Sam sits back in her seat, folding her arms across her chest.

"What do you want from me?" she asks.

"Can you help me?" I ask.

"Maybe."

She narrows her eyes and takes another sip of her latte. Then she gets up and walks away.

"Follow me," she instructs, leading me to the bathroom.

After locking the door, she turns to me and says, "I am going to check if you're wired."

"I'm not," I promise.

"You'll have to excuse me if I don't just take your word for it."

I don't fight it. I'm not wired and I have no intentions of getting the police involved.

First, she goes through my bag, carefully emptying it of its contents and then examining every part of the lining. I don't know anything about bugging devices but they must be quite small if she is so meticulous in her search.

After checking everything that she has dumped into the sink, she turns to me. She begins with my hair, asking me to first take off my scrunchie and then moves down my back and around my torso. She pats practically every part of me including in between my legs, and then asks me to remove my shoes. After checking my ankles, feet, and even the inside of my sneakers, she finally looks up with satisfaction.

"I'm not working with the police. I'm just trying to help my mom," I insist.

"You can never be careful enough in my line of work."

I nod, wishing that she hadn't even mentioned that. The less I know about what it is that she does, the better.

"What do you want to know?" Sam asks.

"How can I get in touch with Marlo?"

"Something easier," she says.

"Do you know people who work for her?"

She shrugs. I take that as a yes.

"Do you know of someone named Shephard Sudler?"

She shrugs again. This time I don't know how to interpret her body language.

"Okay...what can you do for me?" I ask.

Sam takes a deep breath. "Marlo has a lot of people working for her doing a variety of things. I am not aware of everything that she has going on."

"I...I just need to pay her my mom's

debt and that's it. Shephard said that her life is in danger. They're holding her hostage. But I don't want to pay this money to the wrong person."

Sam blinks. I'm not getting through.

"You're the only person I know who actually knows her. I don't know who to trust," I say.

"One word of advice," she says, pointing her finger in my face. "Trust no one."

I nod, looking down at the floor.

"I just don't know what to do. He said they would kill her..." My words trail off.

It wasn't until this moment, standing in this clean sanitized public bathroom that I realize just how much I actually do want to save her life.

When I think of my mother, the memories that flood in aren't of our fights or all the mean names she has ever called me. It's the other ones.

It's waking up to the smell of freshly baked cupcakes one Sunday morning when I was six.

It's her kneeling down next to my bed with me so that we could pray together for

my brother, Patrick, when he was in the
hospital.

It's her running a comb through my
hair and then braiding it in a French braid.

"Your mother has been a loyal customer
of Marlo's for a long time now," Sam says.
My eyebrows rise.

"I had no idea," I say.

"She likes to gamble. And she has won
quite a bit. When she's lost, she has always
paid her debts."

"Do you know where I can find Marlo?"
I try again.

"I can't tell you that," Sam says.

"What can you do?" I ask.

"I can reach out to Marlo and see what
she says."

She pulls out her phone.

"Now?" I ask before I can stop myself.

"I can wait if you'd like."

"No, no, no. Of course not," I quickly
correct myself.

"Wait for me outside." Sam ushers me
out of the bathroom.

Two hours after Sam and I part ways, I
pace around my living room waiting.

Sam makes the arrangements.

Someone is supposed to come to my house and make the exchange.

I am not entirely clear if my mother is being brought here and suddenly, I have a horrible feeling in the pit of my stomach.

What if I made a mistake?

What if I should've believed her when she told me that I shouldn't trust anyone?

What if she's just sending someone here to take my money?

My door buzzes. They're here.

33

WHEN THEY COME...

L ooking through the peephole, I'm unable to believe my eyes. She's here. She's really here. A sigh of relief washes over me.

I open the door and shake Marlo's hand. I've never been introduced to her but given how well known she is in the neighborhood I know what she looks like. I've never seen her without her entourage, but she's here alone.

"I've heard about your predicament," she says. "I'm here to confirm that yes, your mother does owe me fifty-thousand dollars."

Marlo walks around my living room as if she's my mother-in-law, checking on the quality of my living arrangements. Her stilettos make a loud clinking sound on the parquet floors and she wipes her index finger across the bookshelf in the corner, turning up dust.

"Not much for housekeeping, are you?" she asks.

I shrug.

"Don't worry, I'm not either. Still, it's important to know your strengths and weaknesses and to account for them accordingly. That's why I have a housekeeper come by twice a week."

I don't know what to do with this unsolicited piece of advice, so I just smile politely and nod.

She runs her fingers through her ash-blonde hair and then down her neck and over her voluptuous bust. She is one of those people who would exude sexuality even if she were dressed in a potato sack. But dressed in a tailored blazer, dress pants, and a bright pink blouse, Marlo is impossible to dismiss.

"Let's get right to the point, shall we?" she suggests as if I'm standing here making conversation about the weather. "Your mother, Eleanor Kernes, owes me fifty grand."

I nod.

"Will you be paying her debt?"

"Yes," I say. She smiles. "So, where is she?"

Marlo's face contorts into a question mark.

"You are...holding her somewhere," I say.

"What are you talking about?" Marlo asks, crossing her arms.

I furrow my brow, trying to figure out if she is just being cautious in case there's a recording device anywhere in my house, or if she actually doesn't know what I'm talking about.

"Shephard Sudler, the guy who works for you," I elaborate. "He came in here and pointed a gun at my face on your behalf."

"Excuse me?" She takes a step back from me, surprised.

"He said that he's keeping my mom

hostage somewhere, *on your behalf,* and I had until tonight to pay him."

Marlo shakes her head, slowly running her tongue over her bright red lips.

"What else did he say?"

"He said he would kill her if I didn't pay him what she owed."

"You mean, if you didn't pay me?" she clarifies.

I shrug. "Yes, I guess."

Marlo shifts her weight from one foot to another.

"So, why did you seek me out?"

"Because I know that she owes you the money. But I had no idea who Shephard Sudler is. And I wanted to make sure that you were paid so that you would let her go."

Marlo taps her French-manicured nails on the countertop. Her bracelets jingle with each tap.

"You've got yourself a problem," she says after a moment.

"What do you mean?"

"I have no idea who Shephard Sudler is, but he does not work for me. I also did not authorize anyone to kidnap anyone on my behalf."

I stare at her, trying to figure out if she's telling the truth or lying to not incriminate herself.

"Do you have a balcony?" she asks.

"No," I mumble.

"Rooftop?"

"What?" I ask.

"Does this building have a rooftop? Somewhere private where we can talk?"

I nod.

We take the elevator in silence and she holds the door to the roof open for me.

I follow her to the edge and touch the railing.

Instead of looking out into the distance, she walks up to me and starts to pat me down.

"I need to make sure that what we are about to say stays just between us."

I lift up my hands and spread my legs and wait for her to finish. I'm a total stranger and I want her to be as candid with me as possible.

"Why did you take her?" I ask. My voice is despondent and tired.

"I didn't."

My body perks up.

"What do you mean?" I ask.

"What I told you earlier is the truth. I do not know who Shephard Sudler is and I did not authorize anyone to take your mother. She owes me a debt, it's not due back for another week. Plus, she has been a good customer over the years. I'd give another week if she had asked."

My mind starts to run in circles.

So, what the hell is going on?

Who is Shephard Sudler and where is my mother?

"What would you do then?" I ask.

"I never get anyone's family involved in their business dealings. My debtors have to come up with the money on their own or else deal with the consequences."

"I don't know what's going on," I admit.

Marlo narrows her eyes and lights a cigarette. Leaning on the railing, she takes a drag and then turns toward me.

"One option is that this Shephard Sudler found out about your mother's debt, researched you, found out that you could in fact pay her debt, kidnapped her, reached out to you, and now wants you to pay my debt to *him*."

I nod, not really understanding everything.

"But that seems unlikely. If he's this sophisticated of a criminal, he'd probably know that it is unwise to pretend to work for me and to do business deals on my behalf," Marlo says, taking another drag.

Making an O with her lips, she lets out her breath in little puffs.

"The other option, and the most likely one, is that your mother is the one who is behind all of this."

Her words are a punch to the gut.

Even the wind gets knocked out of me.

"She hired some unsuspecting idiot to pretend to be someone who works for me. That guy has no idea who it is that he is impersonating. She wants you to pay her the money that she owes me either to pay

off her debt or to just keep it and start a
new life somewhere."

"You really think she made this up?"
I ask.

I feel the color draining out of my face.

34

WHEN WE TALK...

Marlo's words ping-pong around in my head.

Is she telling the truth?

Is my mom lying?

She has lied about a number of things but never anything this big.

Is she really trying to just steal the money from me? Why?

I told her I would help her.

No, I told her I would help her, but only if she went on the run. If Marlo is telling the truth, then my mother has no intention of going on the run.

"There are two things I can tell you for sure. One is that I did not order anyone to kidnap her or threaten her life. The other thing is that I do not have a Shephard Sudler working for me," Marlo finishes her cigarette and looks around for somewhere to throw the butt.

"There's no trash can up here," I say.

She takes the cigarette butt and tosses it in her purse.

"I never litter," she says in response to the surprised look on my face. "So, what do you want to do?"

"What do you mean?" I ask.

"You have the money. You can keep it and let Eleanor's debt ride. I'll find her on my own, it shouldn't be too hard."

"Or?" I ask.

"Or you could pay it off like you wanted to. Unless, this little development changes your mind about whether or not your mother is someone you should help."

She's not.

I know that now.

I knew that a long time ago.

But ties with toxic mothers are the most difficult ones to break.

We, their children, can never really

fully do it because our mothers never really taught them how to be adults.

We are always looking, striving, seeking that approval that we never got as children.

We don't trust our strength.

We don't trust standing on our two feet.

I saw a therapist for over two years to help me come to terms with everything she has put me through. I know all of these things intellectually, but my heart still aches for her.

"You seem like a nice kid, Olive," Marlo says, walking away from me. We get into the elevator.

"You have a good job. Nice apartment," she continues. "You seem to have your life in order. Why don't you just take that money from wherever it is that you got it from and not get involved in your mother's business?"

I lift up one of my eyebrows.

"Is that your *professional* opinion?" I ask.

"You could say that."

The elevator stops on my floor and I invite her inside.

"It's just for a second," I say. When the

door closes behind us, I ask, "*What* makes you say that?"

"You don't look like someone who has an extra fifty grand laying around. It's probably what you make a year at your job."

"So?"

"Well, people who have that much aren't usually particularly generous human beings. I don't know where you got it but if your mother set you up like this, she's not worth your time."

I take a deep breath and walk over to the kitchen island where I hid the envelopes of money. Before opening the drawer, I look at Marlo.

"If I give you this money will you wipe her debt?"   -

She hesitates.

"She doesn't owe you another cent," I say.

"If you hand me fifty-thousand dollars in cash then her slate is clean," Marlo says with an exasperated sigh.

I hand her the envelopes. She counts the stacks and then points a finger in my face, "You're too good to her. Some people have to learn the lesson the hard way."

I feel like I have to explain.

"She's my mother," I whisper.

"She fucked you over and she'll keep doing it until you put your foot down. Trust me. I know. I had a mother just like her."

Marlo spins on her heels and walks out of the door. I descend onto the sofa wondering if I have made a terrible mistake.

I paid her debt even though she tried to steal from me.

I paid her debt even though she tried to con me.

The thing is that I didn't do it for her.

I did it for me.

I did it to finally, once and for all, be free of her.

35

WHEN HE STARTLES ME...

I f there is one perk to taking your time unpacking a suitcase, this is it, you don't have to pack it all up again when you decide to go back.

I throw in a few toiletries that I took out and dress in my favorite pair of leggings and slip-ons.

My ride share should be here in a few minutes, but since I'm all ready to go and it's a beautiful afternoon, I go to wait outside on the curb.

"Where the hell is my money?" Someone grabs my arm. My body tenses. A couple walks by giving him a disapproving look and he lets me go.

"I had a little chat with Marlo," I inform him. "She told me you don't work for her."

Now, it's his turn to recoil. This is the last thing he was expecting.

"You're in a lot of trouble, Shephard Sudler," I say his name extra loud so that any passerby hears me clearly.

"I don't know what you're talking about. Don't you care about your mother?" he hisses under his breath.

"No, I don't. I have a feeling that none of what you said to me was true," I say sternly. "How much did my mom pay you to pretend to work for Marlo? 'Cause guess what? Whatever it was, it wasn't enough."

My words land like a punch.

I smile at my own power.

Then I look out at the cars driving down the street, praying that my ride will be here soon.

Shephard takes a step away from me, at a loss as to what to do next.

"Marlo is a very dangerous woman to fuck around with," I continue. "She did not like hearing that you were out there using her name to do your bad deeds."

I watch his Adam's apple move up and down as he swallows hard.

"Oh, wait, my mother has no money. You probably did it for free, huh?" I ask.

Talking to him like this is a risk. Just because he doesn't work for Marlo, it doesn't mean that he wasn't holding my mother hostage and wanted a ransom to be paid.

I wasn't sure how I was going to find out the truth about what my mother did but seeing his reactions to my questions, I'm starting to get it.

Marlo was right.

It was my mother who hired Shephard to make the threats.

"Or was she just going to pay you something on the back end?" I ask. "How much exactly?"

Shephard shakes his head and looks down at the ground.

"I've never done anything like this before," he caves. "But I needed money. I got fired and I couldn't find another job for months. My family is getting evicted and Eleanor said that this would be an easy two grand."

Shephard stumbles over his words as he talks and I practically feel sorry for him. Then I remember looking down the barrel of that gun he shoved in my face and my pity hardens.

"There's no such thing as easy money, no matter what anyone says," I say. "You threatened me. You tried to blackmail me. I could report you to the police..."

"No, please don't," he pleads, touching my arm again.

I snap it away from him.

There are tears in his eyes.

"Don't ever point a gun in anyone's face like that again. In fact, don't ever do anything like this again," I say. "Otherwise, I will go to the cops."

"Thank you, thank you," he says over and over, a wave of relief rushing over him.

"But you've got bigger problems than the police. My mother got you involved with some really bad people."

"I thought that Marlo was just someone she...made up."

I furrow my brow.

How could he be so stupid?

"What do you do for a living?" I ask.

"I'm a bus driver. I drive kids to school. They laid off a number of people and all I can get is a substation gig."

Then it occurs to me that it's not that he's stupid, it's just that he's totally out of his element. He has never dealt with the underworld and my mother was selfish enough to put his life and his family's wellbeing in danger for her own gain.

"Marlo is very much real and she is one of the most powerful people around these parts that you have never heard of. It was more than unwise for you to go out there and pretend to work for her. People have been killed for a lot less."

I don't really have any knowledge of this but I get a feeling that it's probably true. Besides, I need to put the fear of God into this man so that he never messes with my mother again.

I see a car with the Lyft sticker on the side pull up to the curb.

It's my ride.

"What do I do now?" he asks. The question catches me by surprise.

"Go try to find a real job," I say. "And get rid of that gun."

"But what if I need it for protection?" he asks.

I shake my head. "I'm the last person you should be getting advice from."

"I know, but you're the only one I can trust. Please tell me."

I shrug my shoulders as the driver puts my bag in the car.

"Is the gun registered to you?" I ask.

"I bought it just for this," he says.

I laugh.

I am not sure that you need that many street smarts to know *not* to use the gun that belongs to you to commit crimes. That just seems like something you could learn from a cop show on television.

"What do I do if your mom comes looking for me?" Shephard asks.

"She's harmless...physically I mean," I add. "But if you do see her, tell her that her debt to Marlo is paid and she can go fuck herself."

36

WHEN I GO BACK...

My flight back to Maui, thanks to the elusive Mr. Crawford, is much more comfortable than my flight here and I sleep almost the entire way there, lying flat on a seat that's almost the size of a bunk bed, in my first class cabin. I wake up rested and refreshed and have time to fix my hair and makeup and make myself look presentable.

I thought that coming here would make me anxious and sleepless but in fact, I feel the complete opposite. Leaving Boston and everything that happened with my mother behind seems to infuse me with energy. By the time we land my worries all vanish and I'm excited to see Sydney.

While I wait for my bags, watching the carousel in the baggage claim go 'round and 'round, I know that seeing Nicholas again should give me some pause. He made an absurd proposal to me, one that only a crazy person would entertain. Yet, a tingling sensation spreads throughout my body at the thought of seeing him again.

Luckily, with the time change, I have the whole day to think about it. I won't be seeing him until this evening.

"Olive!" My mouth drops open.

He's standing outside the double doors, right on the other side of the baggage claim, holding a sign with my name on it.

"I...I thought that Sydney was picking me up," I say.

He folds the paper up and slides it into the pocket of his muted Hawaiian shirt. It hangs loosely around his broad shoulders, but it's not so baggy that it completely obfuscates his chiseled body.

"I asked her for a favor," he says, taking

the handle of my large suitcase away from me.

Left with just the backpack that I took on the plane as my carry-on, I feel naked. When we get outside, the sweltering humidity overwhelms my senses.

He leads me toward a new BMW 8-series convertible in gray metallic and opens the passenger door. I place my backpack in between my legs and fish out a pair of sunglasses to shield my eyes both from the sun and his eyes.

Through the side view mirror, I watch him put my suitcase into the trunk and the way his hair falls into his face with each move. It is only after we pull out of the short-term parking garage that I realize that I've been holding my breath.

"Thank you for coming," Nicholas says, smiling at the corner of his mouth. I give him a slight nod.

"How's your mother?"

I shrug, not really wanting to get into any of the details. "Thank you for helping me. She's fine."

"I'm glad to hear it."

"I don't really know how long it will take me to pay you back."

He glances over at me as we turn onto the winding two-lane highway going along the razor's edge of a cliffside.

"Don't worry about it."

We sit in silence for a while.

I wait for him to say something but then think that maybe he is doing the same thing.

Still, the silence is comforting. Usually, I am very uneasy being in a small space with someone without saying a word, but not with Nicholas.

He has an easy energy to him. He doesn't demand me to perform or pretend. I like that.

"I need you to do something for me," he says as we turn off the main road and into a development.

There is a large gate out front and a security guard who waves us through as soon as he sees Nicholas' identification.

"Where are we going?" I ask.

"You like to play games?" he asks, igniting a spark deep within me.

"I don't know. I guess it depends on the game."

"I think you'll like this one."

He pulls up to a five-star resort and hands his keys to a valet who is waiting out front. Another employee opens my door and helps me out. They place our bags on a rolling suitcase cart and I follow Nicholas to the front desk.

After checking in, they show us to a two-bedroom penthouse suite with a large wrap-around balcony.

"That will be all, thank you," Nicholas says, handing the bellman a tip in the palm of his hand.

"Thank you for staying with us, Mr. Landon. Mrs. Landon. Please let me know if there is anything that you need."

I look out at the impossibly vast ocean through the floor-to-ceiling sliding doors that span the entire west side of the suite.

Nicholas walks up to me from behind. He stops short of touching me but I can feel his breath on the back of my neck.

"Why did he call you Mr. Landon?" I ask.

Nicholas runs his fingers up my arm, sending shivers down my spine. The comfort that I felt only fifteen minutes ago is replaced by a sense of free fall. But I'm not afraid.

"Why am I Mrs. Landon?" I ask, turning to face him.

"Those are our names here at the Wailea Lani Resort and Spa," he says, moving the hair off my neck and bringing his lips so close to mine I can almost feel them on my skin.

I close my eyes to enjoy the moment. I wait for him to come closer. I wait for him to touch me. I open my eyes when he doesn't.

He takes a step away from me, smiling with his eyes. My body yearns for his but I don't dare make the first move.

"In my line of work, I am required to use a number of aliases. Here, I am Mr. Landon and you are my wife, Mrs. Landon."

I straighten my back and broaden my shoulders.

"So, this is the game you *want* me to play?" I ask.

He takes another step closer to me. Tilting my chin up to his face, he runs his finger down my neck. My eyes grow heavy from the anticipation that builds in the pit of my stomach. I move an inch closer, waiting for his lips to touch mine.

But instead he brings them over to my ear and whispers, "This is the game you are *going* to play."

37

WHEN WE PLAY A GAME...

He unzips the garment bag and pulls out a short black cocktail dress.

"What's that for?" I ask.

"My assistant picked it out for you."

"I don't have any shoes to go with it."

He pulls out a pair of nude pumps and unzips another garment bag with his own newly pressed suit. Without even turning around, he begins to unbutton his shirt. Our eyes make contact and I'm the first one to look away. Not really away, more like down. My gaze drifts down his perfectly round pectoral muscles.

Once his fingers unbutton the last button, his shirt falls open and onto the bed. I stare at the way his biceps flex and relax with each move. His sun-kissed skin is perfectly mocha brown. It looks so delicious that I almost want to lick him. My tongue runs over my bottom lip in anticipation.

As my eyes focus back on his, I notice those flecks of gold again. When he smiles, they sparkle. He unbuttons his belt and lets his pants drop to the floor. I get a glimpse of his black, hip hugging boxer briefs that accentuate every part of him.

My cheeks burn and I look away.

"It's okay, you can look if you want to," he says.

My mouth salivates as I stand facing the ocean, waiting for him to put on his suit. I hear him pull up his pants, buckle the belt, and tuck in his shirt. Only then do I feel like it's safe to turn around.

"All decent," he says, cocking his head to one side.

I press my tongue to the roof of my mouth, blocking it from touching my lips.

I know exactly what he's doing.

He's teasing me.

Playing with me.

Toying with me.

He is trying to seduce me. Well, I'm not going to be the one to crack first.

"You look nice," I say, running my eyes over his well-tailored exquisite suit. It fits him like a glove, emphasizing all of his best features.

He sits down on the bed and waits. From the positioning of his body, I can see that he's challenging me. Nicholas leans back on one arm, propping up his head with the other, as if to say, "you wouldn't dare change in front of me like I did in front of you."

For a moment, I consider going into the bathroom for some privacy, but I can't bear to break this sexual chemistry that's brewing in between us. Besides, I want to show him that I'm a formidable opponent. That two can play this game.

With my eyes fixed on his, I take off my cardigan and step out of my shoes. He moves his fingers closer to his mouth and leans a little bit closer to me. I can see his anticipation building and it infuses me with power. Even from across the room, I can feel the energy that's building between us.

I slide down my leggings and let my tank top drop down over my panties. A moment of truth.

A part of me is tempted to turn around for a semblance of privacy but another part pushes me to go on.

I want to make him sit up.

I want to make him stand up.

I want to make him push me down on the bed and kiss me.

I pull my shirt over my head, tossing it onto the floor. He sits up and moves to the edge of the bed. That's a good boy.

I watch him as he looks my body up and down. Without uttering a word, he makes me feel desired.

I reach back to unhook my bra. His mouth drops open and he raises to his feet.

Come on over, I say silently. Put your hands on me. I hold my chin upward, elongating my neck.

He licks his lips.

He walks over. I close my eyes to brace

for impact. But nothing happens. When I open them a moment later, he's standing in front of me holding the dress.

Nicholas hands me the hanger.

I thought that I had broken him, but he turned the game on its head. I tense my jaw and steel my eyes.

He smiles in that self-satisfactory way that makes me both want to punch him and fuck him.

"You remember what I said earlier when I made my offer?"

I take the dress off the hanger.

"Remind me."

"You said that you wouldn't have sex with me," Nicholas says.

I exhale trying to expel the anger out of me.

Taking his finger, he runs it down my neck and then around the outside of my breast and down my side.

"And I promised you that before our time is up, you'd be begging me to do it."

I clench my fists around the hanger until I see the whites of my knuckles. I hate him. I hate him for being right. I hate him for how much I want him.

"Why don't you try on the dress," Nicholas says. He takes a step away from me and sits down on the bench at the edge of the bed.

I shouldn't like the way that he speaks to me but I lose myself in the nuance of *how* he says everything. He makes demands instead of requests and he teases me by seducing me with his gestures.

I pull the dress over my head, slipping it on. I straighten it out in front of the full length mirror and admire how well it hugs my body.

I can only pull the zipper halfway up and turn back to him for help.

Feeling his hands on the small of my back makes every part of me shiver. His hands slide expertly up to the nape of my neck making my head tilt back from pleasure.

Slipping on the pair of pumps that Nicholas' assistant picked out for me, completes the look. I don't know who she is but looking at myself in this outfit makes me want to ask her to be my permanent stylist. Imagine never having to worry about picking out something to wear again. As someone who isn't very keen on clothes shopping, this is a dream come true.

"Your assistant is very good at what she does," I say without taking my eyes off myself in the mirror. "It's a perfect fit and it looks...amazing."

"*You* are the one who makes the dress look amazing," Nicholas corrects me. I smile at the compliment and thank him.

He hands me a small purse and I move some of the contents of my backpack into it, phone, lip gloss, wallet.

"You won't need that tonight," Nicholas says, pointing to the wallet. "Or for the rest of your time here, for that matter."

"Why is that?"

"I'll take care of everything."

"Is that part of the deal that you mentioned earlier?" I ask.

He nods.

"Is tonight part of the deal, too? Me pretending to be your wife, Mrs. Landon?"

He shakes his head.

"Tonight is a trial," he says. "I want to see what you're capable of."

My heart jumps into my throat and my hands get ice cold.

Nicholas walks up to me. He stands so close that I can smell the mint Tic Tac that he has just popped into his mouth.

When I take a step back, I realize that my back is all the way against the front door.

"Who are we supposed to be?" I ask.

"Newlyweds from Boston. We are madly in love and are here on our honeymoon," he says. He takes another step closer to me and I straighten my back against the door.

"Why are we from Boston?" I whisper. My body yearns for his but I don't let myself touch him first.

"The best lies are those that are closest to the truth," he says, touching a strand of my hair and twisting it around his finger.

His eyes drift up to mine and watch me as I watch him lick his lips. I can almost feel the tension that builds between us. I can't take it much longer. I bite my tongue to keep myself from screaming. Give in. Give in, I say. Give in so you can put your hands on him.

His hand makes its way up my neck and toward my lips. My mouth falls open. He runs his finger across my lower lip and whispers, "Tell me to stop."

My knees start to buckle. I can't say no even if I wanted to.

He presses his mouth to mine and a wave of relief sweeps over me.

Finally.

It's finally happening.

I reach out for his face pulling him closer. Our tongues collide, hard at first, and then quickly find their rhythm. I bury my hands in his hair. He wraps his arms around my waist.

I reach for his tie. When I try to untuck it, he grabs my wrists and pulls them apart.

"No," he whispers just as I think he's going to kiss me again. He lets go. My hands drop to my sides.

"What's wrong?" I ask, trying to hide my disappointment.

With a wink, Nicholas says, "We have a job to do first."

THANK you for reading TELL ME TO STOP!

I hope you enjoyed Nicholas and Olive's story. Can't wait to find out what happens next?

One-click TELL ME TO GO Now!

His offer: 365 days and nights = $1 million

My addendum: I'm not doing *that*

His promise: Before the year is up, you'll beg for it

My days of lying and stealing are over, but then Nicholas Crawford makes me an offer I can't refuse. Spend a year pretending to be his significant other in exchange for $1 million dollars.

I tried to put that part of my life, and those hard-won skills, behind me. But I need the money. He needs a partner.

I told him that I'd never sleep with him. He promised me that I would end up begging for it. Now, I want him more than ever.

Especially when I run my fingers over his chiseled body and he **teases me** with his tongue.

Especially when he puts his hands on the small of my back and **kisses me.**

I want him so much I am going to scream. I want him so much...I might even beg.

One-click TELL ME TO GO Now!

SIGN up for my **newsletter** to find out when I have new books!

You can also join my Facebook group, **Charlotte Byrd's Reader Club**, for exclusive giveaways and sneak peaks of future books.

I appreciate you sharing my books and telling your friends about them. Reviews help readers find my books! Please leave a review on your favorite site.

CONNECT WITH CHARLOTTE BYRD

S ign up for my **newsletter** to find out when I have new books!

You can also join my Facebook group, **Charlotte Byrd's Reader Club**, for exclusive giveaways and sneak peaks of future books.

I appreciate you sharing my books and telling your friends about them. Reviews help readers find my books! Please leave a review on your favorite site.

Sign up for my newsletter: https://www.
subscribepage.com/byrdVIPList

Join my Facebook Group: https://www.
facebook.com/groups/276340079439433/

Bonus Points: Follow me on BookBub and
Goodreads!

ABOUT CHARLOTTE BYRD

Charlotte Byrd is the bestselling author of romantic suspense novels. She has sold over 600,000 books and has been translated into five languages.

She lives near Palm Springs, California with her husband, son, and a toy Australian Shepherd. Charlotte is addicted to books and Netflix and she loves hot weather and crystal blue water.

Write her here:

charlotte@charlotte-byrd.com

Check out her books here:

www.charlotte-byrd.com

Connect with her here:

www.facebook.com/charlottebyrdbooks

www.instagram.com/charlottebyrdbooks

www.twitter.com/byrdauthor

Sign up for my newsletter: https://www.
subscribepage.com/byrdVIPList

Join my Facebook Group: https://www.
facebook.com/groups/276340079439433/

Bonus Points: Follow me on BookBub and
Goodreads!

facebook.com/charlottebyrdbooks

twitter.com/byrdauthor

instagram.com/charlottebyrdbooks

bookbub.com/profile/charlotte-byrd

ALSO BY CHARLOTTE BYRD

All books are available at ALL major retailers! If you can't find it, please email me at charlotte@charlotte-byrd.com

The Perfect Stranger Series
The Perfect Stranger
The Perfect Cover
The Perfect Lie
The Perfect Life
The Perfect Getaway

All the Lies Series
All the Lies
All the Secrets
All the Doubts

Tell me Series
Tell Me to Stop

Tell Me to Go

Tell Me to Stay

Tell Me to Run

Tell Me to Fight

Tell Me to Lie

Wedlocked Trilogy
Dangerous Engagement

Lethal Wedding

Fatal Wedding

Tangled Series
Tangled up in Ice

Tangled up in Pain

Tangled up in Lace

Tangled up in Hate

Tangled up in Love

Black Series
Black Edge

Black Rules

Black Bounds

Black Contract

Black Limit

Not into you Duet

Not into you

Still not into you

Lavish Trilogy

Lavish Lies

Lavish Betrayal

Lavish Obsession

Standalone Novels

Dressing Mr. Dalton

Debt

Offer

Unknown

Made in the USA
Columbia, SC
09 February 2024

31621152R00193